Beauty

&

Mr. Rumple

By

Allisha McAdoo

First Printing, 2022

My other paperbacks are:
1. Dark Desires (a collaboration with Thomas J Kline)
2. Playthings with the devil (a short story collection)
3. Mr. Nice Guy (My first novel)
4. Your dirty secret (two of Mr. Rumple's stories.)
5. Night Terrors (A short story collaboration with J.M Swiger
6. Forever together (a vampire novel)
7. Yours for a price (Origin story of Mr. Rumple)
8. Twisted sideways (Asylum short story collection that ties all stories together)
9.T//Error404 (A revenge story)
10. Absurd witch (a comedy

for teenagers under the pen
name Allysha   McAdoo)
11. Corpse Prison (a collection of
stories that star Mr. Rumple)
12.No loose ends (The last
story of Mr. Rumple)
13. Rumple Chronicles (The complete
collection of Mr. Rumple stories)
14. Fatal Tales(a collaboration
with Howard Carlyle)
15. Severed Dick Chili(a godless
exclusive only story)
16. Absurd Witch 2(A sequel to Absurd
witch under the pen name Allysha
McAdoo)
17. Absurd 1 & 2 (A book with both
stories of absurd witch under the
pen name of Allysha McAdoo
18. I'm Cursed(an extreme horror story)
19. I know your secrets (An extreme
horror short story collection)
20. Picture Perfect (A godless
only exclusive)
21. Spiders, Toasters Rootbeer, and other
prompts (My first ever prompt book)

22. Bibliophobia Fear of books (A godless only exclusive)
23. Book of fear (A godless only exclusive)
24. Naughty List (A godless only exclusive)
25. The wrong door (An extreme horror story)
26. Friends Forever (An extreme horror story)
27. Play Hearts (A godless exclusive story)
28. Luckier than you (An extreme horror anthology)
29.The pen (An extreme horror story)
30. Alura (A godless exclusive)
31. Beauty and Mr.Rumple (A sequel to Rumple Chronicles)
Coming Soon
Mr. Yoinks (YA comedy with the pen name of Allysha McAdoo)
Verona (An extreme horror story)
Two Collaborations are in the works as well

My group
https://www.facebook.com/
groups/1718802991696554/
My Facebook author page
https://www.facebook.com/
allishamcadooauthor/
My amazon page (Where you can find my other ebooks on kindle and Goodreads)
https://www.amazon.com/s/
ref=nb_sb_ss_i_4_6?url=search-alias
%3Daps&field-keywords=allisha
+mcadoo&sprefix=allish%2Caps
%2C205&crid=1XQBXSJGNHP0
My author central page
amazon.com/author/allishamcadoo
My Godless.com page
https://godless.com/search?q=allisha+mcadoo
My Tiktok name is allishamcadoo
All paperbacks are available on amazon. All ebooks are available on Godless, Google Play, Apple Books, Kobo, Nook, Pubshare, Kindle

Unlimited, and some titles are available on Leanshare.

Author's Note* I wanted to say thank you for everyone who loved my Mr. Rumple character from the very beginning. You were the inspiration to bring him back to life. However, this is a different sort of story than I normally write. It's not just horror. There are paranormal aspects to it. There are psychological aspects to it as

well. I touched on things that are very deep subjects. I shouldn't have to remind you, that I don't write Dr. Suess. There will also be some grammatical errors, I hope you can see past that and enjoy this story.

Acknowledgment
I wanted to thank a few people. First wanted to say thank to my Mom, Stepdad, and Dre for supporting me. You may not read my horror books but supporting me means so much to me. You keep me from going insane. Thank you for always being there for me no matter what.

I wanted to thank my brother Christopher for always encouraging me to keep going. For always going above and beyond no matter what. Especially for the noods. :)

I wanted to thank one of my best friends Bridget. It's been so many years and you still treat me like I'm someone special for you. Even though we live an ocean apart, you still support me in every way you can. You have such a beautiful soul and it brings me happiness knowing you enjoy my books :)

I wanted to thank a few of my die-hard fans who have made sure to share my work and tell people to give me a chance. You guys are great and I feel so very honored. All the reviews and interviews have really helped me achieve my goal.

And last but not least, I would like to thank all those fuckers who always said, I would never make it in this world. That I wasn't smart enough to do anything or that I would be dead before I reached the age of 17. All the bullies who made my school life hell, and every person who has ever hurt me in some way. I bet you fuckers are eating your words now. So here are my two middle fingers. I will continue to prove you wrong every single day. I know that Karma will take care of you. :)

"You fancy me mad. Madmen know nothing."
~Edgar Allan Poe~

2022

My name is Joannie, and I have a deadly secret. See I am not like ordinary people, and I know what you are thinking, that you hear this phrase all the time. But this time, it holds a bit of truth. I can be described as a beautiful goddess, covered in tattoos of people's faces. Growing up my nickname was beauty and I used to hate being called that. I used to be able to lie and say that the tattoos were from my troop members that died tragically in a war. A war I was never in, but it was enough to get people to leave me alone. I am the result of a deadly mistake I made, so for the most part I avoid people. I don't stay in one place for too long because of the way people seem to look at me. Ever since I have become what I am today, I can't seem to trust many people. For years, I have done my best to keep my secret.

It was an ordinary night that held a nice crisp breeze. I just went for a walk down the town's square to basically observe. Observe the night, observe the people, and just relax. Couples were laughing as they walked hand in hand, and music floated in the air from the street musicians. A couple of small groups were dancing and panhandling. Scenes like that used to bother me, but I couldn't trust myself to get close to anyone. My life was filled with solitude and loneliness. It had to be because of my secret, people couldn't be trusted.

"Miss! Miss! I must draw you!" A deep voice rang out breaking my concentration. I did my best to smile because this man was breathtaking. It had been a while since I had seen anyone like him. I should have walked away. I should have reminded myself that I couldn't have anyone in my life for any reason, not even for sex. His eyes were what beckoned me to at least stop to hear him out. He had the deepest blue eyes I had ever seen. "Draw me?" I asked quietly. "Yes, I draw caricatures. I won't even charge you. I just want to draw you." He said earnestly.

A breeze picked up making leaves dance around my feet a little bit. Surely there couldn't be any harm in letting him draw me? He wouldn't even touch me, my secret would be safe. I got my sob story of the war ready but surprisingly he didn't ask about the tattoos. "Ok, I don't see the harm in that," I said thoughtfully. That should have been a red flag. Everyone I had ever met, asked about the tattoos.

"My name is Matt and my little booth I set up is right on the corner there." He said pointing to a corner that was colorfully lit up with led lights. Without a word I followed him and took a seat on the chair in front of him. He was a tall man with dark olive skin. His hair was kept short and was black as tar. He had no tattoos that I could see but a scar that ran from his eyebrow. It reminded me of the lion scar from Lion King. It made his face look enduring and kind as crazy as that sounded.

I kept chewing on my bottom lip lost in my own thoughts that I didn't realize I had bitten a small hole in my lip. Wincing, I wiped the blood away from my lip and was surprised to see Matt had stopped drawing me. He was sitting there looking at me with a creepy expression on his face. "You are the most beautiful woman I have ever seen in my life, however, I don't know which soul to draw." He quietly said pointing to his canvas. "What do you mean?" I asked nervously, twirling my hair around my finger. I hated the fact that this normal man was making me feel uncomfortable. He pointed at my tattoos, "They are trapped souls no?" He whispered. I glared at him and stood up in a huff. "This is a complete waste of my time, I have other things I need to do," I said smoothing the folds of my short mini skirt.

"Miss, I didn't mean to offend you." He said as he hurriedly stood up. It was too late, I knew I should have not followed him. I felt beyond uneasy. "Not today pal," I said haltingly. I quickly left and threw a glance over my shoulder to make sure he wasn't following me. He stood there by his booth just smiling and even from a far away distance the smile gave me chills. The tattoos on my arms started to pulse and the whispers started to echo in my ears. I took off running, not caring I was in flip-flops."He must die." The tattoos pulsed against my skin. Goosebumps prickled throughout my entire body. "No more!" I whispered back as I threw myself inside my house and started to sob. I hated this, I hated having to listen to the whispers. I knew they were right, it was getting time to add another face to my body. I was supposed to do thirteen souls and I only had nine. I wiped my tears with the backs of my hands and pulled my legs closer to my body. Why did it have to be the one man who managed captured my attention the way that he did? No one had ever done that before. The tattoos whispered Matt's name over and over again to make it sound like a chant.

As I had done so many times before in the past I began to think of how I ended up where I was at today. I was going to find another soul, but it wouldn't be Matt, the first person who realized what my tattoos were. I turned on the fan and closed my eyes to relive my biggest mistake. The fan wasn't keeping up with the massive heat. The heat was the only thing that kept my body from trying to destroy itself. I always hated the heat. The small price I felt like I had to pay for being this way. Sighing loudly, I began to think back on my past.

*****The beginning********
2003

I was barely out of my teen years when I was working at a library. I didn't mind it, it was quiet and I got to spend more time with the books than with people. I grew up with a rough childhood and ended up on the streets by the time I was 15 years old. My stepdad at the time threw me out. He threw all my belongings out onto the lawn and screamed at me to leave. He was threatening to call the cops on me. All because he said I wasn't helping my mother's mental state and I had told him to fuck off. I was rarely home so I knew it wasn't me. My mother had mental health issues that were not being correctly handled by her doctors. The household was very volatile as my mother struggled. I spent a lot of my time working long hours and attending school. I was hardly there, I made sure. Anytime, I was there my stepfather would hit me with leather belts. He would find creative ways to punish me, it was like a game to him. I think he wanted to see how much I could survive. Instead, I didn't say a word as I packed everything I owned into my car. I ended up living on the streets for almost two years.

My stepdad didn't care that I had nowhere to go. Back then, he was a violent man. I was not going to give him any more reason to scar me. I didn't have many friends. I wasn't very liked, people were scared of me. What little friends I did have, wouldn't let me stay with them or their families. My dream library job didn't pay me enough to make ends meet. I couldn't afford my own place so I stayed in my car. I didn't make enough to keep the car running all night, so I wore everything I owned to keep myself from freezing. Unfortunately, I didn't own much. There was still room in my car to lay down in the back seat. My trunk and passenger side were the only things that were filled with my belongings. Then a winter storm hit and I nearly didn't make it. I was so cold and I had walking pneumonia. I worked as much as I could just so I could be in a warm building. By the end of my shift, I was fired for coming to work sick. I needed something to bring in more money and fast. I didn't know how many more winter storms I would survive through. "Why don't you just be a prostitute? You are beautiful. Job sucks, but it pays enough." My best friend Karlie had said during class. Karlie didn't care much about anyone but herself. Her major crisis in her life was when the bus had to take her home from school, which was rarely. She usually called me beauty which pissed me off. Come to think of it, I am not really sure we were good friends. I had never gone to her house to hang out or to have a sleepover. She had never been over to my place and I wasn't entirely sure she knew my last name. To be honest, I think I just desperately needed someone to be my friend. I had already seen how cold the world was at a young age. To me just calling someone a friend was a major accomplishment for me. Karlie was always suggesting for me be put in harm's way. I think deep down inside she hated my beauty. Every morning she look up from her breakfast and smirked. "You look like hell beauty. You won't be luring any guys away looking like that." She said so many times. She never asked about the bruises I tried to cover up. She never showed any interest in what I had to endure on a nightly basis. She never said a word as she watched me wrap up my wrist after it had been snapped the night before. She never offered me lunch when she saw that I couldn't afford to eat much that week.

The thought of men grossly sweating on top of me while fucking me grossed me out. She had told the entire school in a prep rally that my dream job was to be a prostitute and that I was going to legally change my name to Beauty. At the end of the day, I still called her my friend. I kept hoping that somehow she would change and be someone I could talk to, but that never happened.

I spent the rest of the day thinking of ways to survive. I was not going to be a prostitute but I did need to make some money. I had half of a gas tank left with the night temperatures hitting the negatives. By the time school was out, it was sleeting and snowing outside. Taped to my windshield was a small plastic business card. The business card was black with gold lettering on the front of it. The MEC was the front of the card. On the back of it was a black butterfly with blue wings and information. Medical Experiment Center make an appointment today and at the very bottom was a phone number. In the middle of the butterfly, I took a closer look at it and could see dollar signs. I didn't care that it said medical experiment. I should have, I know that now, but I didn't. All I saw were the dollar signs. I guess that would be my first mistake, greed. I thought that if I made enough money, I could get off of the streets. Sure, that probably wouldn't land me in hell, but I was pretty sure that was how anything evil started.

Of course, it started to sleet harder and pelt me with hard pieces of ice. I hurried into the car and called the number on the card with a crappy old cell phone. That cell phone was paid for the minutes as you go, which turned out to be expensive. I only had about ten minutes left on it so I tried to make all phone calls as quick as I could. Back then it was a real struggle. "Hello Joanne, we are expecting you Friday at 6 pm. Be prepared to stay the weekend but absolutely no electronics." CLICK. The person on the other end hung up the phone. I sat there stunned, it was crazy how quickly that call was made. It was almost as if they knew I didn't have enough minutes on my phone. They used my birth name everyone just called me Joannie. I hated my birth name. I played the phone call over and over again in my head. I should have been worried that they were expecting me but a part of me was excited. A weekend stay in a nice warm room and a bed. I had missed sleeping in a bed. I also got the chance to make money? Fuck it would have been nice to get away from the cold, sign me up. I thought to myself.

I hated being homeless. I hated everything in my life, so if there was a pill I could take to erase it all I would. Friday was a day away. I waited till my mother went on one of her drinking binges and my stepdad left, then I broke into my childhood home. I never had a key but it was easy to break in when I had done it millions of times before. I took a shower, washed what little clothes I had, and stole some more canned food and what little cash I could find laying around. There wasn't much of anything because the house had become gross with trash everywhere. It was like my stepdad gave up. When going through his things I found a plane ticket to Arizona. There was only one ticket so I assumed he wasn't taking my mother. Good riddance. I hoped he never came back and I hoped that karma would hurt him like he used to do to me.

I packed up my things again once everything was clean

in my car. I stole a couple of pieces of jewelry from my mother that I knew she wouldn't miss. A part of me was wanting it so I could have something to pawn later on, but the other part of me just wanted to be close to my mother again. My mother had always been my good luck charm until the mental health issues robbed her of her mind. She could no longer distinguish between what was real and her mind playing tricks on her. Then she started to drink heavily just trying to erase it all. I wanted to help her, but being a teenager, I didn't really know what I could do to help. At that time, they didn't teach about mental health in schools. It wasn't a topic no one really brought up. It had been a hush-hush subject. Everyone never said anything about it, and those who did ended up in mental institutes.

I didn't care about my stepdad leaving he was an asshole just like my biological dad was. My biological dad was abusive almost from day one. He tried to drown me and dropped me down a flight of stairs when I was months old. He brutally attacked my mother cursing her for having an evil child. Eventually, he could no longer accept the fact I was alive and my mother wasn't giving me up. He committed suicide while holding me in his arms. What a fucking coward. Most people don't remember things when they are only months old, but I do. I still remember how he was holding me while screaming at my mother that I had to die. He was squeezing me hard and my mother kept trying to get me away from him, but he wouldn't loosen his grip. She had said he was wrong and he needed to die. She gave him a loaded 12 gauge shotgun hoping he would loosen his grip on me enough for me to go to her. I remember him pointing the shotgun toward us both and squeezing the trigger without any sort of hesitation. I could still feel his body slacken as the pellets tore through his chest. Hot sticky blood oozed down my back and somehow I was able to wiggle away and crawl to my mother. He had mental problems and never told a soul until he was looking at charges for molesting his niece. My mother was never the same after witnessing that. Her mental health started to fracture as she struggled to be a good mother to me. I never blamed her. It was hard enough to struggle on your own let alone with a child. I was just not equipped to help her.

My stepdad had taken advantage of her vulnerability. He used it against her. He was no better, he was an abusive prick who liked to torture us both. He used to pretend that he had been in the army and was a drill sergeant. In all reality, he just liked controlling people. He had an insane amount of rules and time limits set for me. If I broke any of them he invented new ways to hurt me. Another reason I worked as much as I could and probably the reason why my mom would drown herself in a bottle.

Since I found very little in the house for money, I decided to put in a couple of extra shifts. I didn't sleep much anymore. Having to sleep out in my car in the middle of winter is uncomfortable. The rest of the time until Friday seemed like it was someone else living it and I was watching from the sidelines. The MEC was located on the outskirts of town by a run-down gas station. Funny how I never noticed it was there before. It looked out of place. It looked like it had just been dropped from the sky. Everything else was in shambles but The MEC. The MEC was modernized and looked like it was expensive. The entire neighborhood looked abandoned and outdated. For a second, I felt like I couldn't breathe. I had never experienced real anxiety before. Every obstacle in my path, I just took it head-on. This place, made me feel unsettled like I should go back to my car and never return. For once in my life, I was unsure about going in a direction.

I grabbed my suitcase I had carefully packed with my school work, a few changes of clothes, some toiletries, and a can of soda I had stolen from my mother's house. I was nervous so I drank the soda like I hadn't had anything to drink in days. My mouth felt dry and there was something about The MEC that made me feel uneasy and I kept turning around to look at my car. I left my cell phone locked in the middle console of my car. I doubt anyone would want something so old and practically a useless money pit. I made sure I hid everything else that wasn't in my suitcase in the trunk. I had a bad feeling and didn't want anything I had to be stolen. When I was satisfied with how everything looked, I made sure everything was locked. I put my keys in a secret compartment in my suitcase. As soon as I walked to the front door a wind picked up from out of nowhere. I had never felt wind like that. It was so cold and it felt evil. I should have turned around and gone back to my car. I didn't cherish the idea of going back out in that wind. I took a deep breath and then walked into the lobby.

It was decorated in black and gold inside the MEC. It had almost a dark feeling to it. The heat was on and it blasted me in the face right when I walked through the door. It was like opening the door to an oven after it had been on for hours. I checked my bag through the security that was standing beside the door. It was a routine check as if it were an airport. They scanned my bag and me until they were satisfied to let me go through. I was a little thrown back about how much security was there. I went through four checkpoints where each one checked my bag and myself for any sort of electronic or a weapon. I had to have a special id card just to get into the small room. It was a heavy-duty id card that looked to be made from metal.

Everything was dark in color as I was led to a small room with only a bed in it. A small man wearing a dark suit came in. "My name is Issac Hyde. Do you suffer from headaches or insomnia?" His voice was deep and didn't match his face. I guess I was expecting some sort of leprechaun voice to come out. "Um, insomnia and headaches," I whispered. I didn't know why I was whispering but something about the man standing there made me uneasy. There was something about his eyes that was unsettling. They looked so dark. I couldn't tell if they were black or the darkest brown I had ever seen. He was staring at me with an intense expression. Just his gaze alone made me feel like the lowest person I could be. I could feel myself shrinking away on the bed.

He nodded. "You will wear your normal clothing and will be getting an iv for fluids. You will remain laying down on the bed while a crown of wires will be placed on your head. You will be injected immediately. We will be monitoring all of your results. Once the results have been analyzed you will leave. Money will be transferred upon your departure. If you fail in any way, you won't be leaving or getting paid. There will be a series of three drugs administered. The first one is for insomnia, called Sleeping beauty. A fitting name for such a beauty as yourself. I wish you the best of luck and results." He pointed to the wire crown and left the room without saying another word. I looked around the room but there was nothing else in the room. It felt so dark and bleak like all hope was abandoned in that room. A sudden wave of what could only be described as depression rolled over my body. I tried to tell myself I was an idiot.

I sat on the bed confused. Did he just say I couldn't leave? I tentatively put on the crown. It was soft wires so it wasn't that uncomfortable to lay down in. I barely noticed the crown, it just felt like a headband. A nurse came in wearing all black including a black face mask. I could see only her eyes but not the color of them. She didn't say a word to me as she hooked me up to an iv. She took a syringe and injected my other arm. She left within minutes of entering the room. She didn't introduce herself and never spoke a single word to me. I don't think I would even recognize her outside of The MEC. This place was giving off major creepy vibes. I pulled the thin hospital-like blanket up to my chin and closed my eyes. I didn't like the sound of the sleeping beauty drug. They didn't tell me if there were going to be side effects or anything about it. Deep down inside, I hoped that it was at least cleared by the FDA to use on people.

At first, I didn't feel anything. Then all of a sudden I felt tired. I closed my eyes for what felt like a second. It took some time to open my eyes. I felt like my eyelids were encased in cement. I felt exhausted just trying to open my eyes. Finally, I was able to crack open just a small slit in between my eyelids. "Wow, you survived!" Isaac said excitedly. "Was I not supposed to be?" I asked. I felt like I had been sleeping for days. My body felt stiff and sore. "All the other test projects failed. All of them died. Except you, you fell into a coma. You have been asleep for two and a half weeks now." I stifled a yawn. "Great. When can I leave?" I asked. I was going to have to come up with some sort of excuse to make sure I didn't lose my job. I looked down at my arms to see bed sores forming. Bedsores? That wasn't supposed to happen after just a few hours. Something felt off.

"You won't be leaving," Isaac said. As he said that, I realized that I was restrained to the bed. Thick straps just above the bedsores were so heavy I couldn't move my arms in the least bit. "Excuse me? No. I didn't fail, nor did I cause you any problems. The agreement was that I got to leave and be paid for taking your experimental drug." I was trying to keep my voice low. I didn't want to show Isaac I was capable of losing my temper. "That was before all the other test subjects died within hours of taking the pill. We have to perfect the pill now to be released onto the market. You have to be the control. I am sorry but that is just the rules. Besides, you still have two more drugs to test. You will have to be injected again with sleeping beauty while we put the finishing touches on the next drug. We need you rested up to the point where we can induce headaches. Got to have a headache to cure it, and too much sleep will do just that." He said in a forced kind of matter. I could tell he was trying to not tell me much.

"I have to leave, I have a job." I thought it was sad that the only thing I had for me outside The MEC was my job. It didn't pay much but I loved to be around the books. Each book was my own personal escape. "I have taken the liberty of contacting your work and have terminated your employment there. Your stepdad has moved to Arizona and your mother is in a mental help center where right now she is drooling down her arm. You have no other brothers or sisters, nor any friends who really gave a damn about you. You have exactly $13.00 dollars in your bank account. You have no pets, no boyfriends, and no home. I think staying here would give you a better future. At least you will finally be important. One more does of Sleeping beauty at its maxim level." He gave in to a small sneer and then left the room. The nurse came back and injected me with something different. This time the syringe was filled with something green. "Excuse me, I have to use the bathroom," I whispered to her. I was hoping she would let me get up from the bed so I could bolt out of here. She acted like she didn't hear me. She just turned around and left after shutting off the lights. This time I felt the temperature drop in the room, and it became clear that the thin blanket was going to keep me warm this time. "Uh, I am cold, can I have a thicker blanket please?" I asked the darkened room. The nurse entered the room walking briskly and tossed a weighted blanket on top of me. It must have weighed at least ten pounds.

I was plunged into a darkness that was so deep it felt heavy against my body. This time I didn't fall asleep quickly, nor did it feel like just a second after I closed my eyes. This time it felt longer for the injection to kick in. It felt painful laying so still in the dark. When I finally drifted off to sleep I was plagued with horrible nightmares. All of a sudden, I was back as a little girl with my biological father. His last night alive was playing on some sort of nightmare loop in my head. I woke up sobbing and begging for someone to hear me. I wanted the light turned back on, I wanted to stop reliving my biological father's suicide. The restraints were digging deep into my wrists and ankles. The light stayed off and the nightmares continued.

I could see a small sliver of light as the door slid open just a crack. I could see the outline of someone and felt a pinch in my arm. The darkness seemed to roll on top of me and I felt like I was being crushed. "No!" I whispered. The person had left and plunged the room into darkness. More nightmares, but these were more vivid and more painful. This went on for a long time. I lost track of time, I lost track of everything. There weren't a lot of moments of lucidity. I knew I was getting injections, but lost track of how many. I felt like my mind was playing tricks on me. Isaac had said only three drugs. This one felt different than the first one and I couldn't seem to break through to real-life again. It was almost as if I had forgotten how to speak. My throat was constantly in a dry state. It hurt more to move my mouth, so eventually, I stopped trying to talk. Each injection brought on a new hell for me while I slept. I tried to keep track in my mind of how many times I saw the slither of light. My mind felt like it became warm pudding mush. The count kept getting lost with each new fresh batch of nightmares.

I could feel every single bit of my body hurting and aching. I could feel the constant throb. Sometimes the pain would be so unbearable that I slipped into darker thoughts. I wanted to die but could still hear the whirring of the machinery around me. I wanted to scream and rip off my limbs to get the pain to go away. Part of me wanted to wake up. This wasn't what I had signed up for and I hated myself for being such an idiot. I should have asked more questions. I should have never come to The MEC.

I lost track of time and bits of my past. Eventually,

the pains subsided enough to where I could open my eyes once more. Isaac was staring down at me writing something down on the clipboard. "Welcome back Beauty. You managed to stay alive for six months. Because of you, we were able to perfect the drug. You have passed the first drug trial and have earned one million dollars. You will get that money when you leave here after the final two drug trials." My head was spinning with all the information he was telling me. I had been asleep for six months? My body was rail thin and was practically see-through. I could see all the veins in my body like a glow highway of blue.

"Why can't I just leave? I don't want to sleep anymore." I just wanted to go back into the real world again. I would work twice as hard to make ends meet. At this rate, I missed my graduation, I missed my job. I wanted to go visit my mom, to make sure she was fairing better. "You are not allowed to leave during the trials. You have two more, both of which won't be putting you to sleep. You may as well stay and make some more money. You will never have to sleep in your car again." He said in a bored fashion as he continued to write on his clipboard.

I winced in pain as I tried to sit up. My limbs were so weak I wasn't able to move much. "Easy Beauty. It will take a few days for you to regain your strength to where you can move. For the next few days, you will try to stand up on your own, eat solid foods and go to the bathroom without any help. Once you achieve those three you can move on to drug trial 2." His eyes were so dark that the light didn't seem to illuminate them at all. "Ok, I will do all that in a day. I just want to get out of here, I'll do whatever it takes so I can." I was hoping to be out of The MEC by the end of the month.

"We shall see. You are showing extraordinary results. Would you like to see the menu from the cafeteria?" He said his dark eyes seemed to search my face for something. This time, I didn't shrink away from him. I was going to do whatever I had to in order to get out of here. I was no longer terrified of him or his eyes. "Yes, I would. I am hungry." I lied. I was far from hungry, but I would force myself to eat. The menu was filled with the most expensive things I had only read about.

I had never tried any of the items on the menu. "I guess give me the lobster nachos," I whispered. I felt dumbfounded. Even as he took the menu away, I still didn't know if I made the right choice. Isaac left without saying a word to me. I spent the time while he was gone trying to move my arms. It hurt so bad and it was a hard task to do. Each arm had 14 bedsores. Dark red abscesses with green pus swimming around each wound. I was able to move one arm that didn't have bedsores around the elbow. Sweat was pouring from my brow and getting in my eyes. I knew I was pushing my body too fast, but I had to get out of here. I would heal properly once I left here.

Now to move my legs. I had to be able to stand and walk around without help. My legs were thin and looked like they would break under my weight. The first thing I tried to do was bend my knees to bring my legs up to my chest. The pain was unbearable and for a second I thought I was asleep again. Eventually, one leg moved slightly. Before I could move it more, Isaac came back with my dinner. The plate was piled high and steaming. Isaac sat the plate on a little table beside me and put it in front of me. Even the silverware was heavily ornate. "You have one hour to eat if you are going to eat," Isaac said then left the room.

It had been so long since I had seen that amount of food. I began to dig in with the arm I could move. It was by far the best sort of nachos I had ever eaten. When I was living in my car, I didn't get to eat much. I tried to tell myself that I wasn't hungry even though my entire body was shaking from hunger pains. The lobster wasn't like anything I had ever tasted before, I had no words to describe it. Before I realized it, I had eaten all the lobster and about 80% of the chips.

I didn't want to waste such delicious food so I continued to eat even though I was too full. I managed to finish the entire plate. Growing up we were poor before I was thrown on the streets like a piece of garbage. We survived on ramen noodles, mac and cheese, and hotdogs. That was the cheapest item of food back then. I didn't own a pair of jeans until my senior year of high school. I had those flimsy stretchy pants with stirrups on the bottom. I got made fun of every time I came to school. We didn't have enough money to even buy a bag of chips. My stepdad had made me get a job when I was 12 years old and forced me to pay rent. I had to buy my own food at 12 years old and pay for my schooling.

The anger for my stepdad boiled deep inside of me. I used that hatred and anger to push myself out of bed. Standing my knees wanted to give out on me. The bottoms of my feet had deep bedsores from the bedpost. One of them burst as I tried to take a step. The slimy blood made me slip a little bit. I fell hard on my knee and I could feel it bruising. I wasn't going to stay in this place any longer than I had to. So I turned back to the anger inside of me. I stood up and walked to the small bathroom beside my bed.

It took me a moment to grab ahold of the sink to make it to the toilet. I fell once more by the toilet trying to figure out how to hold myself up. I thought about my stepdad forcing me to eat the hot sauce he had made when he thought I was lying. I thought about the blisters in my mouth because of it and vomiting up the blood later that night as it hit my stomach. At first, I didn't have to use the bathroom so I sat on the toilet for a little bit. A little bit of urine came trickling into the toilet. I flushed the toilet and went to stand up. Instead, my body came crashing down. My legs were not strong enough just yet to stand.

Upon impact, more of the bedsores burst open. Slimy blood covered my legs and arms. The nurse came in and silently picked me up off the floor. She helped me back to bed and began to dress the many bedsores that were now oozing. I watched her movements and realized that she was kinda sloppy with her bandaging. It was like she hadn't had much practice at all. "Psssst. Will you tell me your name?" I whispered to the nurse. She shook her head no. She pointed slightly to her voice box and shook her head no once more. "Nurse Cindy Rela here can't speak. She had torn out her own voice box after taking a drug at another clinic. She was dumped in a dumpster and left for dead. I found her and nursed her back to health." He gently tucked a strand of hair behind her ear as she continued to wrap up my bandages. Something briefly flashed in her eyes at his touch. I couldn't tell what she was feeling but something deep inside me told me it was a warning.

"You were able to eat but other than .2 ounces of urine you were unable to complete a bowel movement. You won't be able to continue to the second drug trial as of yet. You shouldn't try to rush your progress. Your body does need time to heal." He wrote something more on the clipboard then they both left the room. I wanted to know what he was writing on that clipboard all those times. The lights clicked off plunging me once more into darkness. Fuck that. I thought to myself. I began to slowly try to move my arms and legs more.

I spent more than half of the night trying to strengthen my limbs. I never wanted to get out of a place so fast before. I didn't want to sleep much so I waited until I couldn't keep my eyes open for much longer. I dreamt of my biological dad's suicide again, this time waking up in a cold sweat after shrieking. I woke up to Nurse Cindy offering me a plate of food. It was the biggest stack of waffles with blueberries that I had ever seen. She motioned to a tall glass beside me that held a chocolate shake with whipped cream on top. I nodded and began to eat. The waffles tasted bitter and the milkshake tasted off as well.

I was able to stand up but my stomach started to hurt. It felt like my guts were being twisted into a balloon animal. Nurse Cindy helped me to the bathroom and plopped me on the toilet. The pain was so intense I was trying not to scream. Nurse Cindy passed me a piece of paper and then quietly left the bathroom. "The food was filled with x-lax. I slipped them in there so you can get out of here. No one should be a prisoner here. Flush this note."

I slipped the note between my legs as it felt like my stomach exploded. I was on the toilet for a good 20 minutes holding my stomach and shitting. She must have slipped quite a bit of x-lax in my food. I was happy she was helping me, but at the same time, I felt bad. I signed up for this and I felt like a big baby. I needed to find some sort of inner strength. I knew it was a big risk for Nurse Cindy to help me. I couldn't rely on her to continue to help me. I never thought of myself as being brave or full of strength. As I got bullied and beaten I never thought myself strong enough to go on.

I sobbed quietly into my hands as my stomach violently gurgled once more. At the age of 13, I had done my first suicide attempt. It was the first attempt out of 14 tries. I never told a single soul I was planning on dying. I did everything I could to pick secluded areas but I was always found just in the nick of time. I hated the fact that I had been suicidal. I felt so weak and worthless. Each time that I woke up in the hospital I signed myself out before they got my name. No one contacted my parents, nothing. It was like I didn't really exist to anyone. Loneliness is so dangerous. I was tired of being picked on, beaten up, bullied, and tortured.

Remembering what I had put myself through over and over again caused me to vomit. I glanced over at the small shower that was in the corner of the room. It had been some time since I had taken a shower. I could smell myself and it wasn't pleasant. After an hour, I finally got off the toilet. It wasn't easy to stand up but I was determined to get to the showers. Took me a few minutes but I did finally make it to the shower. I turned on the water and step inside the shower. The water felt weird on my aching body. The bedsores had hardened in some places and the water sounded like it was hitting concrete. The soap and shampoo were bolted to the wall. I had never heard of the brand and it felt like silk over my body. I rinsed off and stepped out realizing I had clean towels and clothes sitting beside the bathroom sink. The mess of vomit had been cleaned up. I slowly made my way over to the towel and wrapped myself up in it. It was an average-sized towel but I had gotten so thin over the years of being on the street. I was able to wrap the towel around me twice. There was a note on top of my clothes. I recognized my favorite outfit and read the note out loud. "Glad to see you have finally showered. You are now ready for drug trial #2. It will start in two days." It was signed by Isaac.

I got dressed quickly with the eerie feeling that he had been in the bathroom while I showered and I didn't notice. I slowly made my way back to the bed and climbed into it. I covered up and closed my eyes. I was beyond exhausted. Thanks to Nurse Cindy I was able to go onto the second drug. I was worried about the next drug. The first one made me sleep so long. What was the second one going to do to me? I hoped that when I woke up I would have the strength to get myself out of this mess.

I woke up to Issac staring at me. "Hello, Beauty. This drug is The Wonderland drug. It's to cure headaches. It won't put you to sleep, however you are the first one to try this particular drug. All results are detrimental. If you experience anything at all you must let someone know. Any results not documented can result in severe side effects. Once this trial is through, you will have earned 5 million dollars." He said studying my face. He produced a syringe that had a purplish hue to it. I held out my arm noticing the bedsores were starting to look a little bit better not like pits of death. He quickly injected me and pointed to a camera that was perched beside my bed. "Just talk into the camera if there are any side effects."

I didn't really know how to feel about being the first one to try out a drug. I had to remind myself that at this point, I was doing it all for the money. That much money could set me up with a brand new life. I would never be homeless again. I felt nothing at first. Nothing but boredom. I had packed my school work but it didn't matter anymore since I had missed my graduation. I wanted to keep my mind sharp so I cracked open a school book. It looked like it was in a foreign language. I rubbed my eyes and tried to read once more. I had completely forgotten everything from my senior year.

I kept trying to decipher the book but gave up once I got a headache. All I could do was write question marks everywhere. My vision started to shift a little bit. Everything seemed to blur into purples and oranges. This headache was reaching maxim pain within minutes. "I have a headache. It hurts. Oh God, it hurts. I thought this was supposed to get rid of headaches, not induce them." I whispered as I slumped down on the pillows. I squeezed my eyes shut and began to work on trying to breathe through the pain. I got up slowly and made my way to the light switch. It took a few minutes and I had to walk with my eyes cracked slightly open. The light was hurting my eyes so much that I could feel tears sliding down my cheeks. As I touched the light switch it sent a brilliant purple spark to my hand. Screaming, I sank down to my knees. My scream seemed to echo in my ears causing the pain from the headache to spike.

The room was pitch black but the cameras had a green glow around them. The slight glow was making my head feel like it was spinning. I made my way back to the bed and before I laid down I said to the camera, "Something is wrong. The lightswitch shocked me. My head hurts. Something is wrong." The pain was so bad that I could barely breathe. I laid down on the pillows that suddenly felt so hard. My hand was throbbing and I could feel my heartbeat in it. Even with my eyes closed, I could still see the shifting of orange and purples.

I wiped a tear away from my face. I cracked my eyes open once more to see it wasn't a tear, but a drop of blood. Fuck! I tried to open my eyes wider but it hurt so bad. I held up my hand to the camera. "I'm bleeding from my eyes." I closed my eyes tightly and tried to will the pain away enough to sleep. I was in too much pain to even think about anything else but the pain.

I heard a quiet laugh to the side of me. I cracked open my eyes and saw that it didn't hurt as much. Sitting beside me was a rabbit's head. The eyes were rounder than they should have been and in the darkness, they looked red. "Why are you laughing?" I whispered afraid my voice would hurt my head even more. "Your crazy ass signed up to be a medical experiment. You volunteered to be a guinea pig. Then you wonder why you are in pain and sitting here talking to a rabbit head. Was your brain dented before the experiment? That drug they gave you is probably cooking your brains." The rabbit head laughed again. I widened my eyes ignoring the fresh batch of pain. "There's a headless rabbit head talking to me," I whispered to the camera. I wiped away more blood from my eyes. "Rabbit head? I have a name you know. It's Alice. Ironic huh?" She laughed.

"Why are you here?" I whispered again to Alice. "To make sure you don't lose your marbles, live through this and don't give up." Alice giggled. "To make sure I don't lose my marbles so my mind made up a rabbit head named Alice?" I asked not caring if my voice hurt my head, which it did.

"Yep, that's right. See any other normal person would have died from the lethal amount that the doctor injected you with. Your body is reacting to the drug because of the bleach you drank when you tried to die. The bleach soaked into your muscles and reacted with the drug. But they can't know that. They will inject you more." Alice didn't giggle and the expression became grave on her face. "How did you know about that? No one knew about that." I said holding my hand over my mouth to muffle the sound. "Why do you think you're alive today girl?" Alice said sternly. "I found you and before you died, I made sure you threw up while you were unconscious. You didn't get all the bleach out of your system. You didn't bother to get the rest of it pumped out by a hospital. You never went to the hospital instead you went to work, where you got fired because of pneumonia. In reality, it was because the bleach and pneumonia made you that sick. That bleach is now saving your ass." Alice said grimly.

"Lethal amounts?" I said closing my eyes once more. My head was spinning. The energy it was taking to talk to Alice was draining me. The pain in my head made it feel like my entire brain was overheating within my skull. I fell asleep but it only felt like a few minutes before I was wakened up by Isaac. "What is she doing?" He whispered to Cindy. I opened my eyes and watched them interact with me like I wasn't there at all. I saw him wave a hand in front of my face like trying to snap me out of a trance."Why is she sitting like that, not saying a word just gazing into the camera?" Isaac said as he checked my pulse. Cindy looked terrified at me. I tried to show her I was awake and ok by blinking. Cindy nodded her head at me slightly to signal she understood. Isaac took all my vitals, squirted water down my throat with a sprayer, and gently laid me back on my pillows. At this close range, I could tell that his eyes were a solid black color. There was no color from his eyes to his pupils. Nothing but darkness in those eyes.

"You can talk, they can't hear you. To them, you are in a catatonic state, except to Cindy. Cindy saw you blink. Your body has put a defense wall to keep from doing more shit to you." Cindy looked frozen in fear as she watch Isaac take my vitals and make notes on his clipboard. I blinked my eyes slowly in a pattern to show her I was ok. "I don't think I gave her enough. I'll have to reinject her in order to get her out of this state. This shouldn't have been a side effect." Fuck. I was already seeing a rabbit head. I didn't know what an upped dosage would bring.

I blinked twice for no at Cindy. She shook her head no at me. There was nothing that could be done that would be beneficial for any of us. This time Isaac injected me with two syringes at the same time. My brain felt like it was exploding. I could feel a scream boiling up inside of me. The sound of his pen on paper was hurting my ears. "NOOOOOOOOOOOOOO!" I screamed as loud as I could. "Welcome back to the living Beauty. I thought I had lost you for a second. I have adjusted the dosage. Any side effects?" Isaac said faking concern. "I told you," I said pointing to the camera. "You didn't say anything or moved after I injected you the first time seven hours ago," Isaac said once more writing on the clipboard. "You better not tell him the truth," Alice whispered. She was now perched on top of Isaac's head. "Oh you know, I was so exhausted. I fell asleep and dreamt that I was talking to you. I feel fine. I have a headache and I feel like I need to get some rest." I pretended to yawn. He looked at me like he didn't believe me.

"You have any hallucinations?" He said peering closer at me. "Nope. I feel great." I said thinly. Alice was rolling around on Isaac's shoulders making faces at him. I did my best not to giggle. He peered at me closer and shined a light into my eyes. "Hmmm, your pupils are a little bit dilated. I am going to give you an iv bag of fluids to help flush the medicine through." Alice was rolling around running her bunny tongue all over the place. It was a hilarious sight and I had to close my eyes so I couldn't see her.

Isaac hooked up the fluids, asked me a couple more questions then left as Alice asked for a carrot. I had never been so happy to be left alone with my own thoughts. "Would you please stop rolling around like that? You are making me dizzy." I snapped. Alice stuck her tongue out and rolled up onto my lap.

I took a deep breath. "You are evil." A raspy voice said to the left of me. I whirled around and saw my biological father standing there. I could see the giant hole in his chest gaping at me like a wicked smile. "I'm no more evil than you." I couldn't stop staring at the hole in his chest. It still looked fresh. I could smell the gunpowder. Alice bounced off the bed and went right through his chest. "Knock it off!" I snapped at Alice. She was really getting on my nerves. "Why are you here?" I asked my biological father. He smiled and moved closer to me. His smile looked wrong like it had been stretched across his face. "Evil girl. You need to be rid of that evil soul within you."

He said coming closer to me. He had his hands wrapped tightly around my throat like a snake. I started to claw at his arms. Bright colors swirled in front of my eyes. I was digging my nails deep within his arm but he wasn't losing his grip.

I moved my arm to angle my elbow to the hole in his chest. I dug my elbow deep into the hole trying to get that bastard to get his hands off of my throat. "Evil girl!" He shouted at me. I could feel my breath getting stuck inside my windpipe from under his hands. My chest felt like it was going to explode. I reached deep inside for strength I didn't realize I had. I was able to shove his hands off of my throat. "What did I ever do to you?" I whispered holding my throat. Out of all the pain from my past, the one I couldn't get over was my biological father.

I was sobbing into my hands. My biological father was chanting the words, evil girl. Alice was surprisingly quiet as I sobbed. My biological father dug around the room and lunged at me holding a scalpel. It was filthy like he just had found it from under a cabinet or something. "You were born evil. Your eyes went from black to blue overnight! You were a strange child that made everyone else look sacred. You shouldn't be alive!" My biological father's face was flushed with anger.

I smacked the scalpel out of his hand and tossed Alice at him. Alice bit him on the face. Alice had big teeth that were shaped like curved razors. Slivers of his flesh were dangling in her teeth and her eyes turned red. My head hurt worse than before. I put my hands on my ears and screamed. "Both of you go the fuck away!" I was screaming until my lungs were hurting. I could feel hot milky blood rolling down my cheeks as I screamed. Once the scream escaped my body, I couldn't stop. It felt good to scream. Nurse Cindy came running in and grabbed my hands.

"I am not evil!" I screamed. I could feel blood leaking from my eyes. Nurse Cindy pried my eyes open with her long delicate fingers. She wasn't wearing her face mask and when my eyes focused. I wish she had left the mask on. I wanted to scream but at that point, I had screamed myself hoarse. She put my finger up to my mouth to silence me. She shook her head no and glanced toward the camera. She slipped me another piece of paper."Don't let him see you scream. He injected you with triple the amount. You are going to be a super-soldier. You are now the pet project." You are the only one that lived. If you scream, he will inject more." I passed the note back to her discreetly. Then she stepped behind the camera and reset it.

She slipped out of the room as the camera booted back up. Where her mouth should have been was nothing more than a nasty scar that stretched from ear to ear. It wasn't a straight line like you would see in the movies. It was very gnarled and twisted. It almost looked like someone tried to melt the flesh back together. That poor woman. Alice was chewing on my biological dad was muttering to himself in the corner. I had to make sure I didn't scream or cause Isaac to come in and give me more. I didn't know what Cindy had meant about being a project pet, but I knew my getting out of this place depended on my silence. I looked around the almost bare room. There had to be something to keep my silence without having to resort to what Cindy went through.

I couldn't find anything, not even superglue to glue my lips shut for a couple of days. When I was a little girl, my biological dad superglued my lips shut. It was only stuck for about a day then the drool from my teething mouth loosened it up. My mother was in the hospital having surgery and my biological father couldn't take any sound from evil mouth. "Ok, listen up," I whispered to Alice and my biological father who was wrestling in the corner. "Quit it."I hissed at them. "For the next few days, I can not be seen saying a damn word. Alice, you will keep me company. You go back into my head where you belong. As for you *father*, you can go back to hell. I turned out to be a good person. We will meet again when I die, however, that will not be any time soon." I smirked at saying the word father out loud to him.

Alice looked at me with blood oozing out of her mouth. "Now!" I snapped. Alice opened her mouth to say something but changed her mind. She began to roll towards the bed crunching loudly on my biological father's fingers. She must have ripped it off while I was talking to them. My biological father leered at me as he shambled over to where I was standing. "I look forward to saving your soul from the shadow that consumes it." He said spitting into my face. Even though he was a figment of my mind, the spit felt real and gross.

"Go to hell," I said making sure to keep my voice down. Seeing my biological father up close for the first time in many years made chills go down my spine. He was still a terrifying person. There was something about his eyes that reminded me of Isaac. They were dark, cold, and unfeeling. I wasn't going to show him how scared I actually was of standing face to face with him. I pushed my hand through the hole in chest and grabbed a hold of whatever muscle I could grasp. "You get the fuck away

from me. You belong in hell." I said making sure my eyes flared with fake confidence. I expected more of a fight but he disappeared right before my sore eyes. Alice was still crunching on his finger but for once was silent.
I felt shaky and slid up onto the bed. Telling my biological dad to go to hell took a lot out of me. I closed my eyes and felt Alice's wet head roll onto my chest. I held her close as I concentrated on my breathing. To keep silent, I was going to have to sleep. I didn't sleep for very long. Strange images merging with Alice's bloody head kept going through my mind.

I would wake up in a cold sweat and force myself to go back to sleep. I was tired of seeing nothing but mangled body heaps in my nightmares but knew I had to remain asleep. Forcing myself to stay asleep wasn't an easy task to do when I wasn't tired. I don't know how long I lay there pretending to sleep. Eventually, I had to get up to go to the bathroom. My legs felt wobbly and to make sure the camera didn't see anything out of the ordinary, I took my time getting to the bathroom. I sat on the toilet wiping away the blood from my eyes. Cindy came in holding a fresh batch of clean clothes for me. I grabbed her hand as she handed over the clothes. "I need to sleep," I whispered to her. I pointed to the scar on her face where her mouth used to be.

She nodded. She helped me dress and gently stuck me in the neck with a syringe she had carefully hidden in her pocket. She helped me back to the bed. The bedsores were getting itchy and sore. I pointed to the bedsores and winced slightly. Cindy slightly nodded and made sure to keep her head down. She began to wipe the bedsores with an antiseptic and then wrapped them carefully in a bandage with medicine on it. The medicine stunk of menthol but the bedsores instantly started to feel better. She left quietly after I thanked her. She returned a few minutes later with a tray of delicious food.

Isaac returned to take my vitals and ask me the same questions. I ate as quickly as I could because I didn't want to have any more medications on an empty stomach. I felt like someone was ripping my insides to shreds but kept eating. The food was bland and tasted as if it all came out of a box. Isaac kept asking me the same questions over and over again for the entire meal. Then all of a sudden he grabbed my arm and stuck me with another syringe. This time the color was a blue color. "Is this the same drug you injected me with before?" I asked worriedly.

"Yes," he said simply. Why was he lying to me? I knew that it wasn't. He was injecting me with something new. He walked out of the room plunging me into darkness before I could even say another word. I could feel my eyes rolling back into my head as I sunk into the bed. Fuck! I don't think Cindy knew he was going to inject me with something new. Oh shit! I was going to overdose and die. Fuck! I tried to roll off the bed, but my body was completely stiff. I tried to open my mouth to scream, but even my mouth stay still. Fuck! I was in big trouble.

I could feel myself drifting off to sleep and I tried like hell to fight it. I didn't want to go into a nightmare that I would never wake up from. "Alice! Help me!" I shouted in my head as I felt my body fall into a deeper state of sleep. "ALICE HELP ME!" I was screaming inside my mind. I tried to find her bouncing head within all the swirling colors but failed. I was falling deeper than I had ever before although my entire body lay still on the bed.

I had to be strong. I couldn't die, not now. I had to live and get out of the MEC. I wanted to get Cindy to a safer place. She deserved that. My head felt like it was full of pressure and was going to split open. I could hear someone vomiting, but couldn't see who. Everything was all shifting colors and mangled heaps of flesh. Please don't die. I whispered to myself as I continued to fall.

Colors merged into darkness, and screams became deeper, as I continued to fall. I tried to stop myself from falling but my body refused to listen. The screams are echoing and my body feels like it is being pricked with a thousand ice picks. In the darkness, all I can see are red dots. Then, I realized it wasn't red dots I was seeing, but eyes. Red eyes connected with horribly mangled rat faces peer at me. "Alice!" I whispered in my mind. I was hoping that somewhere amongst the rat faces was the rabbit head I was searching for. With that word uttered, it seemed to bring the rat faces alive. Before I could move away, thousands of rats started to attack my body as I fell deeper and deeper into this hole in my mind.

I could feel each bite from the rat as they scratched at my body. "SOMEBODY, HELP ME! I DON'T WANT TO DIE!" I was screaming inside my mind. I could see myself still laying on the bed with my arms tucked tightly against my chest. I wasn't moving and I couldn't tell if I was actually breathing still or not. More rats jumped out of the darkness at me. Sharp teeth started to tear at my flesh. "LEAVE ME ALONE!" I screamed. As I fell, I shoved what felt like thousands of rats off of me. I could hear them hitting the hard concrete below me out of my sight. I could almost hear the thuds their huge bodies made as they landed on the concrete. I assumed that this falling would eventually come to an end, and I would also be hitting that same concrete the rats were.

I needed to wake up but the two drugs that were injected into me were clashing. I had always read that if someone was close to death they would see their life flash before their eyes. I didn't see my life, nor was there any sort of bright white light. All I could see were mangled body parts now raining down on top of me as I fell. When was I going to hit that concrete below me? At this point to get away from the mangled debris I would gladly welcome the concrete. I just wanted to stop falling. I wanted to wake up. How was I going get back to my body that was so stiffly just laying there like nothing was wrong? I tried to scream but nothing came out.

All of a sudden I started to fall faster. The wind was whipping at my face and arms like it was made from knives. I was afraid that the wind was going to shred me to pieces. I looked down at my arms to my sides and thought I saw stitching all over the place. As the fall quickened, even more, I thought I saw the stitchings slowly become unraveled. I was going to fall apart before I reached the bottom. I tried to tuck my body into a tight ball as I fell so the stitchings wouldn't continue to unravel. Each time the wind whipped at me, I could feel tears rolling down my face.

My tears were cold as they hit my neck. Suddenly, everything felt cold. Too cold. I was shivering and falling faster. My arms looked like I had been in the deep freezer too long. I had a bluish tint to my limbs. The pain coursing through my body felt like I was being zapped by an electric current. When the mind goes cold, it's hard to think of anything else but the cold. I tried to think of my life but all I could think of was turning into a human popsicle.

I kept my body curled up into a ball. The stitchings were frozen and my fingernails were turning purple. Being too cold is a horrible feeling, just like starving. Your body turns up the pain dial on your body as it freezes. The more I struggled to keep myself warm as I continued to fall, the colder I got. I could see my breath in front of my face in a misty fog.

I could see something below me it looked to be the ground of an old bunker. I tried to straighten out my body so I could try to land on my feet. Broken legs would be better than a broken back. My body wouldn't budge. I was frozen in such a tight ball that my body refused to move. I was going to land hard and probably shatter my spine. I tried to make peace with it, telling myself that I deserved it. I had tried to give up so many times before. This time I volunteered for the experiment. I wanted to close my eyes but found I couldn't even blink my eyelids. My tears had frozen them open.

Right before I hit the bottom, I felt a sharp jab in my right arm. Something wasn't right. I landed on the bottom but it gave away into something soft. It felt like it was made entirely out of the softest blanket ever created. The floor covered me like it was a blanket then slowly I started to ascend up. I was no longer falling but somehow I was floating back up. I glanced down at the floor as I rose up from it. I could see pictures of my past playing on the floor like it was a movie. The pictures were in no order just random snippets.

Falling went so much faster than floating to the top. I was

still cold but the higher I went up, the warmer I got. I could see the stitching that was all over my body rot away very slowly. The colors returned brighter than before but this time there were no rats. Just materials that looked like it was from inside someone's body. Everything looked like it was flesh and blood. The pain in my body seemed to erupt from everywhere. Sharp, stabbing pain that would take away my breath as it ran rapidly through my body. My muscles were tingling with a cramping sensation.

When I opened my eyes, I could see Cindy leaning over me. She was holding a couple of syringes in her hand. She looked at the syringes then looked at me and held them up for me to see. I picked the bright blue one that I had seen Isaac inject me with. She looked horrified. She held up the syringes again, and I nodded once more choosing the blue one. She tucked the syringes into her pocket and made the sign of the cross with her hands over her face like she was praying. She was holding back tears when Isaac came into the room. "Congratulations! You passed The Wonderland drug test! You have one more to go. When you leave here, you will have a total of 46 million dollars. We are making great progress. The last drug administered will be every 4 hours for five months. This drug is a cure-all type of drug we call The Sea Witch. These are supposed to be the miracle drugs to cure everything, even cancer. Hopefully, it will heal up those bedsores. Since it is a cure-all, we will be injecting you with dangerous viruses firsthand. Once the virus is running rapidly through your body, you will get The Sea Witch. We will repeat this until the five-month mark documenting which viruses we were able to cure, which ones were only able to be tamed and which had no effect." Isaac said happily.

"Wait, there is a possibility that you are going to make me sicker and this drug won't cure it?" I asked horrified. "Don't worry, you are the star of the project. We will make sure nothing happens to you." He smiled but his face did not light up with warmth. It was a cold, twisted, smile. Behind him, Cindy slightly shook her head no. Before I could ask any more questions he stuck me in the neck with a syringe. Fuck. I have no idea what was going to happen to me now. I had no idea what I was injected with. Cindy and I paid real close attention to the syringe that Isaac was preparing. The liquid was a dark red color. Cindy started to shake and slipped to the floor. Isaac paid her no attention as he plunged the syringe deep into my arm.

For a second his dark eyes turned a blood-red color as he roughly held my arm. "For fucks sake Cindy get up off the floor." He said in an irritated manner. Cindy slowly stood up and pointed to her kneecap. She made a twisting motion with her hands. "Ah, your knee is fucking up again. If you need to go ice it for a few that's ok." He said softening his tone. Cindy nodded briefly and slowly began to limp towards the door. I could tell the limp was exaggerated but held my tongue. Isaac turned his attention back to me. "I have to inject you with a booster to speed up the virus." He said softly. He grabbed a syringe with green fluid. I looked over at Cindy to see tears going down her face. She shook her head no slightly. Tears were falling faster down her face as she quietly left the room. The red syringe was bad but whatever the green one was, it was worse.

Isaac gently picked me up and put me on the bed. He covered me up with a thick blanket. This time, he left the lights on. "I'll be back in an hour." He said as he wrote down the time on his clipboard. The door clicked shut behind him. I felt too warm and tried to kick off the blanket. I felt like the temperature had reached a high level. Sweat formed thick beads along my forehead. I had started to sweat through my clothes. It seemed like the lights were searing into my eyes.

I got up slowly from the bed and made my way to the bathroom. I was splashing water on my face to try and cool down. I sank to the cool bathroom floor for a minute. I knew I had to get back in front of the camera so Isaac could have his results. The bathroom floor felt so cool. I couldn't seem to get up off the floor, it was the only thing that kept me from sweating so much. I felt like I was melting into a puddle.

My veins were starting to turn black and I could see them through my pale flesh. It was like a highway of twisted dark paths all over my body. I picked myself up off the floor and stepped fully clothed into the shower. I let the icy cold water run over my body until I felt like I could go lay back down on the bed once more. I didn't bother to dry off and climbed back into the bed. I was cool for about five minutes then I felt like I was boiling in my body. My veins got darker to the point where they looked like a child written all over my body with a sharpie.

My body felt stiff as I tried to get into a more comfortable position. Sweat was pouring from my body so much that the bed now had a sweat outline where my body had been. I couldn't stay in the bed, I had to go back to the bathroom floor. It was the only cool place. I got up slowly and swayed unsteadily. I tried to steady myself but found myself tangled up in the bedsheet. I fell hard on my wrist.

I couldn't tell if it was broken because I was sweating so much. I tried to hold my wrist but the sweat just made my fingers lose grip. Sweat was pouring into my eyes so I couldn't tell if it was bruised or swollen.

I could see Isaac coming into the room. "It's so hot in here," I whispered. I tried to stand up but couldn't get a grip through all the sweat. Isaac came and lifted me up under my arms. I could tell it was a struggle. He put cold compresses on my entire body until I was starting to feel better. "The heat part is about to be over with. Hopefully, that will be the only nasty side-effect." Isaac said. It sounded blurry because of the sweat pouring into my ears.

He had to change out the cold compresses several times because my body heat kept melting through it. He offered me a drink of what looked like ice-cold water but it tasted something too sweet to be water. Instantly, I began to cool down. Whatever I was drinking helped bring the sweating down. I was beginning to feel like a normal human being again. Once I was cooled enough, I began to feel tired. "Rest up, because, in an hour, you will be given The Sea Witch," Isaac said writing more than usual on his clipboard. "Wait, that wasn't The Sea Witch?" I asked. I was dreading his answer. "Of course not. That was only the virus and the booster to make it more prominent. The Sea Witch will be next. Then you won't get any more injections until The Sea Witch cures the first round of viruses. Since this particular virus is brand new and has not been released to the public. We will not be sure what you will be doing. You could be feeling great and you will have access to the gym and pool. You could be feeling shitty in that case I'll be here to document everything and help keep you alive. With each injection, your probability of surviving drops. So, rest up Beauty." Isaac said turning back toward the door.

"Don't call me Beauty," I whispered to his back as he left. "Of all the fucking nicknames in the world. Why did I get stuck with the one I hate?" I grumbled to the camera. I was going to make sure I stayed alive no matter how low my odds were. I closed my eyes, forcing myself to sleep. I braced myself for any nightmares that were coming my way. Maybe I could grab strength from them. I was going to need all the strength I could get. I was going to have to get Cindy to safety when I got out of here. No one should ever be treated like Cindy.

Nightmares didn't visit me while I slept. I was still very aware of my surroundings as my eyes were closed. I never did fall into a deep sleep. Eventually, I gave up trying to rest and began to do a small workout. First I did some stretches then I began to jog in place. Issac came in and wrote on his clipboard before he said anything to me. "You can stop now. It's time for The Sea Witch. Please have a seat on the bed. Once injected we will bring you a small dinner. It's not a great idea to be injected on an empty stomach. However, just a fair warning this dinner will be packed with carbs and protein. Which will be your new diet while you are on The Sea Witch. You must finish your entire meal every time you are fed. If you don't keep up with the carbs and protein, there's a small possibility that The Sea Witch will start to eat your body from the inside. If that happens, you won't be able to continue your study. You will forfeit any and all rights to get paid. On the day of your last shot, you will legally be declared dead. You won't be able to return to your old life. You will have a new identity and a new place to live. You will leave here in a brand new car registered to your new identity. You will tell no one about this drug trial. If you even mention a single thing from this trial, you will be hunted down by my boss. You won't take too kindly to anyone who tries to alter the tests in any way shape or form. After you leave this place, you will have a check-up appointment four times a year. It will never be the same place, you will get an appointment card two days before your appointment. Failure to go to the appointments will result in consequences. Those consequences will be a price too high to pay. You will get a job offer given that you survive. Make no mistake it will be a top-secret government job. You'll get paid and get upgraded to The Ultimate drug. That will turns your bones into metal and your flesh impenetrable. Do you understand these conditions?"

Isaac said with an icy tone. It was a lot of information to take in. I would no longer exist after this last drug trial. "What about my mom? Could I make sure she is taken care of at the best facilities?" I asked hoping to sound brave. The entire ordeal was beginning to sound like the end of my life. "Your mother has died as of last week. She overdosed on the medication she needed to keep her split personality at bay. Your stepdad and half-brother were killed tragically in a car accident on the way to Arizona. All your friends or lack thereof have graduated and moved to other states." His voice held no warmth or comfort. "Do you understand the conditions?" He asked me one more time. "Yea," I said quietly.
He nodded and then began to prep my arm for The Sea Witch injection. I watched him stick the needle deep into my vein feeling only a slight prick. "Why the names?"

I whispered as I watched him slowly push the plunger down on the syringe. "I didn't name them. My boss had a daughter and she had wanted to name the drugs. She died after catching a stray bullet at a mall along with her mother. To honor his daughter's memory, he chose the names she wanted to use. Once they get onto the market, the names will be changed into something more professional. No one outside this facility will know the nicknames. You need to eat as soon as possible. Cindy will be in here about five minutes." Isaac pushed me onto the bed so I could lay down.

True to his word, Cindy came in holding a big, metal tray in her hands. On the plate were the biggest steak I had ever seen and a gigantic portion of pasta. I looked at Cindy who nodded at me. I had taken a sign language class in high school so I asked her if she knew sign language. She nodded once more. We kept our signing conversation to a bare minimum. She pointed to the gravy boat for the steak. On the side that the camera couldn't see, was a small note taped. I thanked her for the gravy and poured a good amount onto the steak. I was able to get the note off with a fingernail. I carefully hid the note under my leg. I ate quickly and then went to the bathroom as she carried my tray out of the room.

Sitting on the toilet, I read her note. "You are doing good. You are the only one in 157 studies to live. Keep doing what you are doing. Keep an eye out for the color of the syringes. I saw his notes and halfway through he is going to give you something called a Diablo. There is a way to speed up this last trial. You will have to ask him to inject you within a week of this last injection. You will have to put your body through Hell. When I can, I will inject you secretly with something that will keep these drugs from killing you. You now have the attention of the entire military and government. You must continue to be alive. The gravy that will be served with each meal with being full of something to keep your vitals stable. One way or another, you will leave this place." I ripped up the note and flushed it down the toilet.

I didn't feel comfortable with Cindy putting her life at risk trying to help me. Isaac didn't seem like the type of person who wouldn't pass up a chance to hurt someone for disobeying him. I took a quick shower and got dressed in clean clothes. I brushed out my hair and realized it had gotten longer. It was now past my waist. How did my hair grow so fast?

I started to braid my hair down my back to get it out of my face. I was bored. I started to work through the school books I had brought with me. When I first started working on them, they seemed like they were too hard. Now, I had been working for about thirty minutes and finished half of the book. I kept checking my answers in the back of the book. All of them were correct to my surprise. I kept working and saw that my hands were shaking. I had finished the entire workbook within an hour.

I tossed the book into the trash. There was no reason to keep the books. I wouldn't get graduation. Everyone had already graduated. The world thought of me as dead. Sighing loudly, I began the next book. I finished it quickly and threw that one in the trash as well. I had one more book left. I was still bored. I worked quickly through it and Isaac came into the room while I threw that book in the trash."I'm bored." I said to him. He nodded. "I will bring you some materials to work on. The first part of The Sea Witch seems to be improving your cognitive functions. Hopefully, it will continue to do good things for you. The second part should be kicking in soon." He said thoughtfully. Within minutes he had brought in shelves and started to fill them with big books. I now had four shelves filled to the brim with books. He stacked notebooks and pencils on the table beside the bed. I hoped the second part of The Sea Witch would boost me up some too instead of hurting me. Isaac hooked up a small patch to the side of my forehead. "This will be able to tell us your brain waves while you are working through the books." He said simply. It felt like a sticker on the side of my forehead.

"I'm hungry," I told Isaac before he left the room. He looked at me with disbelief and nodded. Cindy brought in another tray with the same thing I had for dinner. I grabbed her hand and shook my head no. I handed her the gravy boat. "I don't like the gravy," I said then began to eat the meat and pasta. She looked shocked. I closed my eyes concentrating on the meat until I heard her leave the room. I would survive without getting her into trouble.

I began to slowly work through a book. It was a college medical book for those who wanted to be the top doctor. I began to write notes. If I was going to survive this, I will have to know everything my body will endure. Eventually, I got stiff sitting on the bed. I got up and tried to stretch. Every single bone in my body cracked horribly loud. Curious, I took my finger and bent it all the way back to my hand until I could hear it snap. It didn't hurt much. I pushed the finger back until it was set back into place. It felt like someone had been squeezing my finger too tight, not like it had been broken.

For the next month, I ate all the steaks, refused the gravy and studied as my life depended on it. I filled up a total of 112 notebooks. Isaac put each finished notebook in a bag of my things to take out of The MEC. I practiced breaking a bone then setting it back into place. I worked out to the point where sitting still was painful. The next month came the second virus. It made me hungry and want to throw up all the time. I lost some weight that I had gained during that first month of being on The Sea Witch. The second dose of The Sea Witch was stronger. I kept working through the books and then giving myself quizzes on everything. I am surprised that I retained any information at all. Given how hungry and nauseous I was.

The third virus made me feel so weak. I couldn't move so throwing up became a difficult task. I could see my skin tightly across my bones. I felt sicker than I had ever been before. Nothing stopped the hunger feeling. Food had become my enemy. The more I wanted, the more it made me sick. The sicker I got made me try to fight harder to stay alive.

The fourth virus made me depressed. More depressed than I had ever been in my entire life. I could no longer focus on the books. I had stopped vomiting but I didn't want to eat. Cindy came in several times offering milkshakes and candies. I would suck on the hard candy and I would feel great. I had a feeling that Cindy was helping me with the candy. That lonely feeling started to eat at me from within. I spent my time thinking about ending everything. No one would ever miss me. I lost more weight. When Isaac weighed me, I had gotten down to 90lbs.

"You need to eat!" Isaac said in a cold tone. I sat there dully looking at him. I didn't care to eat. I gave up. I couldn't even bother to shrug at him. "If you don't start eating, I will have to take drastic measures." Cindy came in holding a tray. Her hands were shaking as she handed it to Isaac. "What is the point? Just kill me." I muttered. Isaac slapped me hard across the face. It was the first time since I arrived at The MEC that excessive force was used. My cheek was stinging and I could still feel the heat of his hand on my face. Cindy lunged forward and caught Isaac's hand in midair as he was going to hit me again. Isaac's eyes glinted with a rage that I had never seen in a person before. "Start eating NOW!" Isaac hollered. I grabbed a small piece of steak and tried to shove it into my mouth. The texture was off and it felt like mushy leather. I started to gag but forced myself to swallow the piece of the meat.

Isaac slapped Cindy to the floor. "LEAVE HER ALONE!" I screamed. I jumped off the bed to help Cindy off of the floor. "Well, it looks like if you don't eat, I'll hurt her." Isaac snickered. I was starting to really hate him. "You have four minutes." He said setting a timer on his watch. Cindy was silently sobbing as she picked herself off of the floor. I grabbed the steak and took a huge bite. The steak tasted awful for once. I didn't want Cindy hurt anymore so I kept shoveling huge bites into my mouth. I was vomiting and pushing the food down my throat. At one point, I had to push the vomit and steak back down with my fingers.

Every time vomit would escape my mouth, Isaac would slap Cindy again. I finally managed to get the entire steak down. He brought in another steak. "I can't eat anymore." I whimpered. My stomach was starting to hurt. "You've lost too much weight and now the study is at risk. You will eat until you make weight again." Cindy stood silent and wiped away her tears. She was rigid. My hands were shaking as I tried to reach the steak. As my hand was outstretched Isaac stuck a syringe into my hand. I tried to jerk my hand away but the syringe got deeper.

Cindy made a muffled sound. I looked at her to see her put her hand over where her mouth used to be. "There, I'll make sure you gain the weight now! You will not ruin all my work!" I tried to stand up but instantly fell down. Isaac pulled me up by my hair and flung me into bed. I felt paralyzed. He grabbed Cindy and brought her in front of my face. "I did this to Cindy. I took her mouth. She was a test subject who tried to save another patient. I finally realize that she has been helping you as well." I had never seen Isaac act like that. Isaac broke her neck so fast that I almost didn't see it happen. I started to scream and Cindy's limp body landed on top of mine. Her eyes were wide with shock. I tried to move, but couldn't and before I could say anything, I fell into a deep sleep.

I was back in my nightmares again. This time my biological father, Alice, and Cindy all merged together. They became this horrible blob of flesh and teeth all mashed together like a failed science project. I still felt paralyzed even in my dreams and the merged blob kept trying to bite off pieces of my flesh. I felt sharp pangs in my arms. I felt like I was being weighed down by waves of pain. The more I struggled to get away from the horrendous blob, the sharper the pangs in my arms got. Then I woke up.

My arms were bleeding in several different places. Cindy was lying beside me with her neck at a 90-degree angle.

Isaac was grinning from ear to ear. The smile made me feel like something worse was about to happen. It was nefarious and cold, something I wasn't used to seeing. When I tried to sit up I realized he had strapped me to the bed.

"Here's the deal Beauty. I have transferred the entire amount of money for all the drug trials into your account. You are free to leave as soon as you consume Cindy's entire body. I have given you your final injections. I skipped the last viruses and The Sea Witch. I gave you The Ultimate and The Diablo. You no longer have a choice but to accept the offer of a job. I told the board that you didn't survive. You belong to me. If you survive and consume Cindy you are free to go. You will come back when I call you to serve me as Cindy did. You are my secret weapon in case the state decides to pull my funding." Isaac said quietly. "Consume her?" I echoed. "As in eating her? I can't do that! I am not a fucking cannibal!" I said not bothering to keep my tone down. "Oh, see that's where you are wrong Beauty. The mixture is going to give you some pretty unique side effects. The only thing you don't have to eat is her hair. You are going to be strapped to this bed until you can't take the hunger anymore."

"Why would I do anything you tell me to do? I'll just let you kill me too. May as well, I have nothing to go back to when I leave this hellhole." I tried not to sound too hopeless. That's what I felt, was completely hopeless. I hated who I become and my depression was worsening. Why did I sign up for this fucking stupid experiment?

"Because I have lied to you. Your mother is still alive. She could really use your help in getting into a facility that will treat her better. Besides, I will tell everyone that you killed Cindy. All it takes is a couple of buttons and the footage from that camera will show you killing her. I will make sure you end up in prison where they treat freaks like you bad. You will do this, you do belong to me and you have less than a month to consume Cindy. If you don't, I'll keep injecting you with all sorts of things I've created." Isaac laughed. His laugh sounded like razor blades scraping on a chalkboard.

I couldn't say anything. I didn't know what to say. "I can't eat another human being," I whispered as giant tears splashed down my chin. "Another lie. All those steaks were made from superfoods and the dead patients who didn't survive the trials. Rather than have to tell the state that the trials have been unsuccessful, I lied to make sure I didn't get shut down. According to all my paperwork all those people you ate, survived, and are doing great in the trials. So yes Beauty, you can eat a human. Only this time, I am not going to spend the time to turn dear ol' Cindy here into a steak. You will consume her raw. I wouldn't take too long if I were you, however. The body begins to break down and decay pretty quickly. You wouldn't want to eat slimy, skin that tastes like acrid trash. You are to eat all of her organs except for her eyes. I have a whole room with nothing in it but jars of eyes. The best part is that I use that room for the patients who think someone is always watching them. It's hilarious." He laughed. There was something wrong with his laughter. It sounded off, different and inhuman.

"Why are you suddenly acting this way?" I asked as I drew my knees up to my chest. My arms were stinging but resting them on my legs made me feel a little bit better. Not much, just enough to not focus on the pain. "Because

Beauty, I have injected myself with a drug that should grant me immortality. Besides, I have noticed that when you are enraged, depressed, or just fed up with everything you provide better results. Just think of me as Dr. Jekyll and Mr. Hyde. You started out with the nice side of me, but now that the world thinks you're dead and I can do what I please, you get the real me. The real me hates people like you. Now you are wasting precious seconds asking me questions. That body isn't going to eat itself you know. Every second that body lays there it's going to start breaking down and decomposing."

Right before he left he pulled out his cell phone from the pocket of the jacket. He showed me a picture of my mom tied to a bed with men all around her looking down at her in an evil manner. "Tick tock. I don't know how much longer your poor mother will survive in those conditions. I hear that she isn't just a fuck toy but a torture toy as well." He made sure not to move the phone away from my face until I could see every detail of my mother's pain. Glaring at Isaac I reached over to Cindy's arm and took a bite. Ripping the flesh away from the bite was a bit of a problem since most of my teeth were flat on the bottoms. I didn't let that stop me. I used my nails to help cut the skin away from the tissue and muscle. As I was chewing he showed me another picture on his phone. This one was from my bank account and that money had been deposited earlier that day. "Enjoy your meal Beauty." He snickered and walked towards the door.

"DON'T CALL ME BEAUTY!" I screamed at him. "I will end you just you watch." I glared at him. I could feel the blood of Cindy dripping down my chin. "See? That pure rage is going to be wonderful. I can practically taste that promotion!" Isaac gleefully said as he skipped out of the room. I looked at Cindy and closed her eyes. "I'm so sorry," I whispered to her. I had to get out of The MEC. Suddenly, I felt like I had some sort of purpose in life. I finally understood why heroes in movies did everything in their power to solve the situation. I was no hero but come hell or high water, I would be a villain.

I kept ripping away at her flesh and muscle of Cindy. I felt like I was going to be sick but after a while, I just pretended it was day's old chicken I was eating. I kept seeing my mother in the picture like it was burned into my brain. I could see the misery in her face. She may not have been the best mom growing up, but she was still my mom and didn't deserve anything she was going through. Isaac didn't bring me anything to drink so I had to drink Cindy's blood. After a while, however, the blood started to taste stale and felt more like leftover oatmeal. It no longer quenched my thirst.

I had dug to her bones in her arm. Around the joints looked like she had spam jelly on them. That God-awful jelly-like preservative that came from meat in a can. I hated spam. My stepdad always used to make me eat without cleaning off that jelly first. Sighing loudly, I told myself to stay strong. I started to snap off bones then did my best to scrape out the marrow with my fingernails. My fingernails were now caked with gunky flesh and blood. It was like using a dull spoon to dig rather than a fingernail.

I felt so full that my stomach was starting to really ache. I wasn't going to take my time with this. I had to eat her quickly so I wouldn't be caught eating a decaying body. To break up the horrible fact that I was eating a dead human body, I read the rest of the books. I was barely able to keep the flesh and tissue down but forced myself to do so. I wanted to make sure that Cindy didn't die in vain. She had helped me in so many ways and helped kept me alive.

I had never eaten so much in my entire life. My stomach was starting to protrude like I was pregnant. The more I ate, the more I tried to get my mind off of what I was doing. If I was to be a weapon then I was going to be the best damn weapon I could be. Eventually, my plan was to take out Isaac Hyde once and for all. I wouldn't just stop there, oh no, I wanted to take out the entire corporation that thought it was ok to experiment on people. I wanted the fuckers who thought it was ok to kill off people who probably had struggled their entire life just like I had done.

By day three, the skin on Cindy was becoming beyond slimy. It smelled horrible and the blood had congealed into a thick paste that reminded me of that jellied cranberry sauce people served on holidays. I had never tried it and after eating Cindy, I don't think I could ever want to try it. The bone marrow had started to break up slightly making it oily and not good tasting. Every time I looked up from a book I would make sure I flipped off the camera for Isaac to see. He didn't bring me anything to drink so for the first few days I drank out of the sink like an animal. But eventually, he found out what I was doing and turned off the water to the sink. I tried the showers next, but the water was so scalding hot that I couldn't get a proper drink. "I need water!" I hollered at the camera.

Isaac didn't come and bring me any. I was not about to die after all that I had endured. I fashioned myself a small paper cup and dipped it into the toilet. I tried not to think about all the germs that were in the toilet and focused on the fact that the water was decently clean. By day seven, I was hallucinating. Everyone that I had ever met in my past had shown up at one point to stare at me while I ate Cindy. The bullies in my school jeered at me and tried to make me feel horrible about what I was doing. Their voices were the only ones I didn't tune out. I let that anger for all those years course through my veins like it was on fire.

I'll show them all once I got out of The MEC that I was not a loser. In order to survive my plan for revenge, and to survive the world on the outside, I was going to have to be the beast.

Day 13

I had almost finished with Cindy's arms and legs. I could no longer pretend that it was a different kind of food. The smell of the decomposing body was enough to make my stomach constantly dry and heave. My stomach hurt all the time. I was getting fatter and crazier by the minute. I took off my pants because they were starting to fit snugger than I wanted them to be. At this rate, it was going to take me a month to finish her. The rot and decay were so hard to eat. "Why don't you at least bring me a damn fork so I can eat better? I have no more fingernails to dig with." I said to the camera. Every single one of my fingernails was broken and scabbed over. I made sure I only slept about four hours a day so I could hurry up and consume Cindy. Isaac came in holding a plastic pitcher of water and a plastic fork. "Really? A plastic fork?" I picked up the fork not caring about his answer. I tried to scrape off the flesh with it but the prongs broke. "Can I have a real fork?" I sighed. "Can you be trusted with a real fork?" Isaac said as he pulled on out of his shirt pocket. "What am I going to do with the fork? Stab you in the dick with it? Just give me the damn thing so I can finish this." I was in no mood to deal with his crap.

He hesitantly handed me the fork and I glared at him as I took it. I kept eating and willing my stomach to stop bubbling with nausea. He was talking to me but I wasn't listening. I didn't care. Nothing he said meant anything to me anymore. I had a goal in mind and nothing was going to stand in the way. He took my vitals and continued to blabber away. "Just go the fuck away so I can finish Cindy. Your voice is grating on my nerves. Do what you came to do then leave." I no longer was hiding my rage. Isaac wrote something on the clipboard and came closer to me. He lifted my chin up to stare at my eyes.

He was asking me something but I didn't hear him. I started to dig into Cindy's torso. It was slimy and smelled like a rank skunk but I kept eating. The nice thing about a decomposing body was I no longer had to chew through the flesh. Everything was so mushy that it slid down my throat. I could see her organs now all of which were tinted green. Fuck it. I stabbed the organs and began to chew on them. Even decaying, they weren't as bad as I thought. My stomach still didn't like it, however. It didn't stop me from dry heaving with each mouthful. The heart was the best it was so tender. The vocal cords reminded me of string bean sprouts. They had a horrible taste and felt a little like celery. Isaac was still in the room bothering me. It was pissing me off, he was being more attentive than normal. I decided the only way he was going to leave me alone was to eat Cindy's eyes. I stuck the fork deep into the eye socket and scooped the entire mess into my mouth. I could hear Isaac roaring but it didn't stop me from doing that to the second eye as well.

He was trying to pull my arm away from Cindy's head but it was too late. It was time for the brain. I shoved the fork into her forehead as hard as I could several times until I heard the crack-like ice cracking on a frozen pond. Isaac kept pulling at my arm to get me to stop so I shoved him away from me until he went flying back. I started to eat Cindy's brains as fast as I could while Isaac was trying to pry me away. There was nothing left but the spine and the back of her head.

I threw the fork down onto the floor in front of Isaac. "I am ready to leave now," I said in a matter-of-fact manner. I stood up and felt dizzy. I moved to try and get past Isaac. I felt this massive pain in my arm. I looked down to see a tattoo of Cindy's face appearing. "What in the fuck?" I screamed as I slid down to my knees. "I tried to stop you. When you consume a human the way you did including the eyes and brains their face will tattoo on you." Isaac said wiping the blood away from his lip.

"Why? How the fuck do I get it to stop?" I put my hand over the tattoo that was still being created on my arm. "It's one of the side effects. It's something so rare that no one has ever heard of it. You should rest up for a couple of days while I figure out a way to stop it." Isaac said as he stood up. "No way, I want to get out of here. You promised me! Figure it out and call me in a month." I had already wasted enough time in The MEC. I tried to get dressed but nothing fit anymore. "One night here and I will make sure you leave with better-fitting clothes. I need to run a few tests so I can figure this out." Isaac pushed me back to the bed. "Just rest please don't make me give you a sedative. I don't know how your body will react." For a moment he sounded concerned. Four men that looked like they ate bodybuilders for breakfast came strolling in. They removed what was left of Cindy's remains and began to quickly clean the room. "Compile a list of the books you wish to take with you. You can choose up to 8 books. The rest will be saved for the future." Isaac said as he began to hook up some machines to read my heart rate. I carefully selected the 8 books I wanted to keep. Books I knew would help me in my future for revenge.

The men cleared out the books. My stomach still hurt and laying down sounded good. "Don't try to keep me longer than a night." I hissed at Isaac. I cautiously got onto the bed. "Don't worry you probably won't be resting tonight anyway with all the tests I will be running. By 6 am you will be leaving." Isaac said over the roar of machinery. "Can I have a cellphone while I wait?" I asked. "Yes, but you will get no signal until you leave this place. But you can play games or read to pass the time." Isaac said.

One of the men gave me a cellphone that was still in the box. He plugged in the phone and then gave it to me. In his hands, the phone looked tiny. It was a top-of-the-line phone and was huge in my hands. I turned it on and started the process of bringing it to life. The date on the phone is automatically set. "Isaac is this date right? The phone says it's 2013." I had to repeat myself a couple of times to be heard over the machinery. "That is correct." He said as he nodded to the men who were clearing out everything in the room but the machines Isaac was working on and the bed.

"2013? I was supposed to graduate in 2003! That's ten fucking years in this place!" I said angrily. Isaac shrugged. "Your trials took the longest time. You outsurvived over

300 people who registered the same time you did. You get a fresh new start tomorrow at 6 am." He made it seem like it was no big deal. To Isaac, it probably wasn't a big deal to him. I lost ten years of my life and that was something I couldn't wrap my head around. Tears were sliding silently down my cheeks as I tried to find a game that would keep my interest.

I did everything I could to figure out everything I could that happened in the last ten years. But to tell the truth, the world hadn't changed much. I ended up playing a mystery game that made the time go by faster. I finished the game and still had two hours to kill. Isaac was looking exhausted and was moving faster than before. "Ok, I am done. In exactly one month I'll call you on this phone. You can add anyone you want to this phone, however, all calls will be monitored. It's like a company phone so keep that in mind."

Isaac disconnected the machines and the ringing in my ears intensified. I hadn't realized how noisy the room was until it went quiet. Isaac came into the room with new clothes and a set of car keys. "Get dressed. It's 6 am and I need this room. Remember one month. Company phone, you better answer it." Isaac said a little forcibly. I quickly got dressed in the bathroom. It wasn't the prettiest thing to wear but anything was better than what I had been wearing for the past ten years. My arm still hurt where the tattoo was. The keys felt heavy in my hand as I walked out the door.

Two out of the four men that cleaned out the room I stayed in for ten years helped me out to the parking lot. One stayed by the front door and the other one helped me to my brand new car. It was dark blue and the nicest car I had ever seen. "Remember ma'am this is a company car. It has your new place to live already programmed into the GPS. I'm not supposed to tell you this, but Cindy was my sister. She wanted me to tell you that the house is under heavy surveillance. She left you a present in the suitcase you brought with you that is hidden in the trunk. Usually, Isaac burns people's stuff they bring with them. She was careful enough to hide your suitcase where the spare tire goes. There is an on/off switch by the right headlight that will allow you a two-minute window to get it out without Isaac knowing. Go to the house and park this car there. You can stay at Cindy's house which has never been discovered by anyone within The MEC. In her present are directions to the house as well as the keys and deed to it. It will all be under your name. Make sure you spend a couple of nights in the house The MEC watches. If anyone asks, you are just out partying. Also, I overheard Isaac say to the head chairman that the tattoo of Cindy's face will never be able to be removed. It's permanent. He is going to want you to kill 13 people, their faces tattooed on your skin will be the proof. Normal tattoos can be easily detected and removed. So try not to fool anyone. Thank you for keeping hold of my sister's soul and not letting Isaac get his hands on it. That's why he takes the eyes. He is trying to use you to resurrect someone from hell. If you kill the 13 people and do what Cindy has told you in her present, you might be able to turn it around onto him. Getting rid of Isaac and The MEC in one shot. Play along and act dumb for now. But make sure the bodies you consume, are of the vilest people you can find. The worst kind of people will be easy to turn towards him. I know it's a lot to take in. You are stronger than you know. Kid, you survived almost a thousand people who have died since the project started in 2000. When it comes time for the final showdown and you take care of all these fuckers, be sure to set my sister's soul free. You'll have to brand yourself to make sure her soul can't be released from the tattoo. Find yourself a witch, and bind my sister's soul to you. That way you can set her free. She will help you along the way as much as her soul is able to. Take care, Ma'am." He gave me a pat on the back and hurried back inside The MEC.

It was a lot of information to take in but this time I was ready. I was glad Cindy hadn't died in vain. I didn't trust many people but Cindy and her brother were two people that I would. I got into the company car and began to drive to my destination. It had been so long since I listened to music. All my favorite songs were considered old now. It's ok, I thought to myself. I was older as well as much as I didn't want to admit it. I turned up the stereo and rolled down the windows grateful to feel a breeze. I felt like I was in prison and had just been released. Everything was different.

I knew I was going to have to lay low for a week or so before I could see what Cindy put into my suitcase. The house was a small two-bedroom house. It was pretty and fully loaded with everything. It had furniture, and food stocked. I turned the second bedroom into an office and put together a few bookshelves. I had managed to retain almost all the knowledge from the books I read while I was at The MEC. I was pretty proud of myself for being able to put together bookshelves with no problems. Since I knew The MEC was watching my every move I got into the habit of going for a jog in the mornings.

During my jogs, I would go into stores and do everything

I needed to do. I started a waitressing job so that way I would have a cover. I had made friends with the dishwasher guy named, Norris. He was able to get my money onto a secret bank account that The MEC couldn't touch. He made it look like I never touched a dime in the account The MEC set up for me, even though it was bone dry. With my new account set up, I was able to buy myself a brand new cellphone and laptop. The laptop was heavily encrypted so I would be able to work on it without detection. I also bought myself another car. This car I left in a storage garage so The MEC wouldn't know about it. Next was to get the suitcase out safely. That would be tricky to do. I had an idea it was crazy but I knew it would buy me the time I needed. I picked an oil change place that was super close to the storage.

I drove the company car in for an oil change and tire rotation. While they were working on that, I disabled the camera in the truck and quickly got out the suitcase. Then switched it back on and closed the trunk. "I have to run a few errands I will be back in about an hour. The oil change guy smiled and nodded then began to work on the car. I ran the mile and a half to the storage and carefully hid my suitcase in the car. Everything was ready to go for when I would go to Cindy's house. Now it was time to train so I could get ready to kill the 13 people I needed.

I went back to my car and drove to a few stores. I used my personal debit card which I had them personally make it look like my card from The MEC so they wouldn't be suspicious. The only difference was a small gold star in one of the corners of the card. I bought a laptop and several books to go into the office at The MEC house. I knew they would bug that laptop instantly as soon as it came inside the house. I turned the rest of the house into a gym. I got rid of the furniture except for the bed. I kept the kitchen the same. In order to train I would have to lose the excess weight, I put on.

I hated looking at myself in the mirror so I turned all the mirrors around in the house. I was finding myself falling into depression more and more. I had to stay true to my mission to get rid of Isaac and The MEC. Deep down inside, I knew that I would never really accept the way I looked. While I was at The MEC house I decided to apply for my GED. Then maybe enroll in some college classes.

After about a month, I decided it was time to go to Cindy's house. I waited till it was my usual time to go for a run and went to my car in the storage. I unlocked my suitcase and found Cindy's present. She had written me a letter, along with the keys, deed to the house that she signed over to me, and a book. The book had a math cover on it but that was a fake cover. The book was called Rumple Chronicles by Allisha McAdoo. It was a fairly hefty book but each page was covered with a holographic covering. I stuffed it all back into the suitcase and drove the directions to Cindy's house.

It was a beautiful house that was out in the middle of nowhere. She had put a 6ft fence all around her property with barbed wire on the top. Her place had the best security, including security into Isaac's office. She had plenty of weapons, secured rooms, and an indoor swimming pool. I brought my suitcase into what she had turned into her office. It was covered wall to wall with monitors that watched over her house, The MEC house I was currently at, and Isaac. I sat down to read her note.

"Joannie,

If you are reading this, then Isaac finally has killed me. Please use my house for your own. My brother will explain things to you as you leave The MEC. I didn't have any children, and both of my parents were killed. My brother has made sure that no one carries on our bloodline. Everything I have belongs to you. You are the strongest woman I know. You survived things that no normal human being ever could. You have earned my respect which I don't give out to just anyone. The book is about how you are going to defeat Isaac and The MEC. The holographic pages will confuse the cameras. You will see the real words but the cameras will only see math problems. This way you can study at the other house as well. You have a tough journey ahead of you, but you can't be scared. More people will die if you don't stop them. You have been injected with so many serums at this point that your intelligence surpasses anyone else I have ever met. Never trust Isaac. Play along, play dumb, pretend you have amnesia, and do what you have to do in order to win this war. You have literally become a superbeing.

Don't be afraid to tap into yourself. Be that person you need to be in order to take out the evilest organization in the entire world. You have had it rough, but that will help you to continue to survive. There is a small key on the keyring that belongs to the house keys. Go to the Midwest bank on Maasonry Drive. There is a safety deposit box inside. All you have to do is tell them your name. They will be waiting for you. I did some extra steps to make sure that you would be taken care of once I realized that you survived when no one else did. You are to take all contents in the deposit box. It will all be in a black bag that you will bring here. Do not bring it to The MEC house. You will need what's in the box to help get Mr. Rumple. Mr. Rumple is our only chance.

Mr. Rumple was carried off to hell, it's going to take a miracle and you. Always be mindful of the cameras, don't involve anyone who you are afraid to get hurt. Also, your mother is not alive. Isaac used that to fuel the anger inside of you. He broke into her home and put a syringe of something horrible in her. You can look for her obituary online. It said she died of a heroin overdose. Another lie. Isaac and The MEC have covered up thousands of murders. Your mother is buried under the name Marina Johnson. She is buried underneath The MEC which is located in Missouri. There is a MEC in every state and some overseas. Isaac oversees about 90% of them. I had my brother tap into all of Isaac's feeds. Whatever he sees so will you. You won't be able to stop anything at first. You must get stronger. Keep track of everything he does, and learning his routines, it will come in handy. Take care of yourself. I'll always be with you.
Love,
Cindy"

I carefully straightened the note and glued it to Rumple Chronicles on the inside under a blank holographic page. For the first time in a long time, I felt like I was in a place I belonged. I would not let Cindy die for no good reason. Cindy had provided me with passports and fake documents. I had both the original and the fakes. All that meant was I needed a disguise for when I had to use my fake documents. Cindy also provided a kit that had colored contact lenses, wigs, makeup, and even a tattoo I could put on as a scar. She had thought of everything.

I glanced at the fake name that she had provided for me and rolled my eyes. Beauty Beastson. That was my new name. "Hilarious," I whispered to myself. A nickname I have always hated was going to have to be my alter ego.

The next day I went to the bank and told the bank manager my name. He nodded and gave me a strange awkward hug then led me to the secure room. I inserted the key into the box he provided for me. True to her word, there was a black bag inside. I didn't bother to look into it just stuffed it into my backpack. "Thank you so much." I headed back to Cindy's house. I opened the bag and realized it had everything I needed for some sort of ritual. It also had syringes that Cindy had carefully marked. Each one was to keep my body strong and not fall apart from all the crap I was experimented on with. She must have stolen thousands of them. I was only to take half of the syringe once a week. I carefully hid the bag in a place where no one would find it in a million years.

For the next year that became my life, switching between the two houses, studying for school, and for how to get to Mr. Rumple. I trained every single day pushing my body as far as it could go. I did half a syringe once a week like I was supposed to and was beginning to feel great. I still thought myself fat and ugly but I knew that wouldn't change. I had to push those thoughts to the side and keep with my training.

I went back to The MEC to find that it had completely imploded. There was no evidence that a facility ever was there. I did my best to keep my two lives separate from each other. I answered Isaac's calls every time. I played dumb and went to all his stupid meetings. I let him take my vitals. Thanks to the syringes that Cindy left for me, they weren't what he wanted to see in my vitals. The calls became fewer and fewer as he concentrated on something else.

I finished reading the book Rumple Chronicles. The author had killed off Mr. Rumple and sent him to hell. I sat back in the chair in The MEC office. How in the hell was I going bring back to life someone who had been killed and sent to hell? I was not a necromancer by any chance. I remembered the bag that held ritual stuff. Ok, so I was going to have to find a ritual. For that, I would have to go to Cindy's house. I kept her house just as she had left it. I couldn't bear to move any of her stuff because she died helping me.

I got dressed to do my "jogging" when my company phone rang. "You are no longer needed for the studies. Your contract is ended. You have ten minutes to leave the house, the phone, the keys, and the car there. The house is set to explode in exactly ten minutes. You are not to have any contact with The MEC again. Thanks for your service." Isaac hung up before I could say anything. I could hear a beeping that kept getting louder and louder. FUCK! I grabbed everything I could and start packing as quickly as possible. Luckily I never cared for the furniture. I was able to stuff everything I owned into a couple of suitcases and a backpack. I made sure to not leave anything behind. I found the multiple bombs throughout the entire house. I could tell they weren't fake bombs. These were complex and looked expensive. Probably how they were able to remove The MEC from the location I remembered.

I flipped off every corner I could that I remembered there was a camera and made it outside just before the place exploded. I was just far enough that the blast didn't hurt me. The sound of exploding glass and metal hurt my ears. I kept walking with my things. I was able to catch a cab and paid the cab driver to take me to my "mom's" place. I had him drop me off about five miles from Cindy's house just in case I was being followed. I walked around for about seven miles then right before I hit exhaustion I snuck into Cindy's place. I made sure everything was locked, loaded, and secure before I showered. I fell asleep sitting up in an armchair.

I woke up around 3 am and saw on the news that The MEC had covered up the house blowing up. They had told the news that I was carelessly smoking a cigarette not knowing that the gas was off on a stove. When I clicked the stove on to light my cigarette it instantly blew me up. I saw them wheel out a body all bloody and cut up. They were saying that was my body. Another failed experiment I was presuming. They would go to extreme lengths to say that I died. Fine, it was time to just go by Beauty. I still fucking hated the nickname but Cindy had set it all up for me. Probably to remind me what all I endured under the care of Isaac Hyde. As much as I hated it, I would make sure I lived up to it because of Cindy. I felt bad about how she died and blamed myself constantly for it. I needed to make it right.

I looked through every page in the Rumple Chronicles until I discovered a bit of a map through the stories. Cindy had a huge whiteboard so I began drawing every place I knew of in Kansas. If I was going to get into Necromancy I was going to have to go to the old asylum place. Mr. Rumple's final resting place. According to the map and what little I could find on the internet, I realized it was about a six-hour trip for me. His final resting place was on the other side of the state by Missouri. I found it interesting that Mr. Rumple's final resting place was only a couple of hours away from The MEC's headquarters.

I spent a few hours weeding through the fake sites on Necromancy. There were so many fake sites my eyes were starting to hurt. Just when I was about to give up, I found what I was looking for. I had to verify I was 18 and that show proof that I wasn't going to be calling back from the dead my grandma. That one was tricky. All I could think of was to find my grandmother's obituary on my phone and show the site that picture. She had died in the '50s. Mr. Rumple had died just shortly before I entered The MEC. According to the site, he would still be accessible, but to enter Hell, I would have to have a near-death experience. I would have to do something horrendous to make sure I arrive at the gates of Hell. I had to make sure that I had someone bring me back once I captured Mr. Rumple.

I first had to kill 13 people, before I could do anything. Cindy had said to really embrace my superbeing. I didn't see myself as a superbeing. It was time to get myself to get close to the vilest people I could find. I was smart enough that I was able to get a couple of online degrees. I finished a four-year college in under two months. I joined MMA, so I could learn to hurt people. I was already a decent fighter but I needed to be the best I could get. Things were different now that I had been experimented on so to speak. I could no longer feel pain like I used to do. The only thing that fueled my rage was everything that Isaac had done, or is doing. It's amazing how much you can do when you can no longer feel pain.

I was warned there were going to be side effects to the injections. Feeling any pain of any sort was no longer a thing for me. I took a knife and stabbed it through my hand until it got stuck on the table. Nothing. I watched my blood slowly trickle out of the wound, but it didn't bleed like it should have been. That was the first side effect I noticed. The other side effect was every once in a while, I had a hankering for human flesh. After I moved into Cindy's house completely and the world thought I was dead, I gave myself a makeover. I went to a bar, had a little too much drink, and tried to take a guy to a seedy hotel. I just wanted sex. I hadn't had anything good since my freshman year.

I had lost my virginity in a cramped car parked in an abandoned industrial park. It was hardly something I was proud of. Years later, I found out that the guy I lost my virginity to turned out to be a pedophile. Nothing made me feel sicker than finding out that. Sure, he was older than me. I was only 14 at the time and he was 18. So, I wanted a meaningless moment where I didn't feel sick to my stomach thinking about my first encounter. But by the time, I got to the hotel, I was no longer interested in sex. I wanted to eat him. I left him in the bathroom taking a piss and I took off running. I would have to save my hunger for the vile people. Not drunken one-night stands. Drunken one-night stands would not help me get rid of Isaac. When I got back to Cindy's house, or at this point, I should start calling it my house, I was sobbing. I was frustrated beyond frustration at that point. I wanted somewhat of normal adulthood. Every time I got an urge like that, I worked out until I could barely move.

I still felt ugly and fat, even though my body was nicely

toned with muscles. I had less than 3% body fat and after years of being treated like shit, I still felt like I needed to carve away my imperfections. I wasn't sleeping really well, caught myself sleepwalking a few times. I got my hands on a rare book of Necromancy and a rare book about Hell. They became my bedtime stories. I had every single page memorized. "Time to get food." A voice whispered to me shocking me. I was alone or at least I thought I was. I checked every single camera there was no one with me. "Time to kill."The voice whispered once more. My arm started to throb and I realized it was Cindy whispering to me. I was incredibly weirded out but knew she was right.

At first, I took to the streets at night like batman to look for some vile people. I was definitely no batman and found no one. I decided to work smarter not harder. I paid a visit to a couple of prisons and talked to the wardens. I paid them for the vilest people they could find. Money well spent. I took their most dangerous criminals off their hands and they delivered them to me. They would drug them up well so they couldn't wake up or hurt me in any way. I think they did that because I was so pretty. Eating people was a hard thing for me to do. There was so much I had to do to get them prepared.

I think what I hated the most was shaving every single hair, eyebrow, and eyelash off of each body. Next, I would drain them completely out of blood. I would donate the blood to the red cross and other blood banks. I would donate them after hours so no one could connect the blood to me. I found I didn't feel any sort of emotion chopping up their bodies. When you have as much money as I do, you can buy the best tools to chop up a body.

Without blood in the bodies made things so much easier. I would grill up all the organs including the brain. Those taste much better grilled. Everything else got put through a meat grinder with a hamburger. The eyes were something hard I couldn't figure out the best recipe for.

The eyes tasted nasty and I hated when they would burst inside my mouth. For some reason, the eyes always tasted of rotting eggs. The first couple of criminals I ate I had to duct tape my mouth shut so I wouldn't vomit up anything. I needed their souls. Swallowing my own vomit has got to be the absolute worse thing. The stomach acid mixed with the vomit would burn the hell out of my throat. Afterward, I would lose my voice for a few days and be sick with a sore throat. No amount of cough drops or sore throat remedies helped.

I made sure I ate everything cooked and as quickly as possible. I was not going to have a repeat what happened in The MEC. After I finished each person the tattoo of their hideous faces would painfully appear on my arm while I tried to sleep. The nights that the tattoo would appear would keep me awake for the rest of the night. I caught myself sleeping during the day and waking up in strange places. One day I woke up in a tree and had a severe burn on the arm that didn't have the tattoos. I never figured out what caused the burn.

It got to the point where I had to literally chain myself to a support beam in the house. 14 locks and chains so tight it would cut into my skin was what it took to keep me from wandering around. The worst thing happened one night while I was chained to the support beam. I could see on the cameras that some sort of weird swat team was creeping around Cindy's house. I couldn't take the risk of being discovered. I quickly unlocked the locks and packed everything I needed. Then I set the entire house on fire. There was an escape hatch under the floorboard that led to a storm drain. I excited out with the few bags I had and locked them behind me. I could hear the entire house exploding and people screaming as I continued to run a couple of miles to the storm drain.

Time to start my life over. This time I chose a nice quiet town in the mountains. I had always lived in Kansas and would miss it terribly but I needed people to forget about me. I live in the mountains for about six months before deciding to move to Florida. Florida was where Isaac moved to according to an anonymous tip I received. I had a feeling it was probably Cindy's brother but couldn't be sure. Once in Florida, it was easy to find him. I stayed in the shadows until I met Matt.

2022

I had been sitting on the floor for far too long because my entire body was stiff. I was covered in sweat. I needed four more souls and I needed to get a move to resurrect Mr. Rumple. I felt like I was running out of time. It was time to get the hell out of Florida and go back to Kansas to the spot where Mr. Rumple got sent to hell. I was so fucking tired of this relentless heat. I went back outside hoping to catch some sort of breeze. My hair clung to the back of my neck and t-shirt like it was a wet dryer sheet. Luckily for me, there was a man trying to hurt a woman in an alley not too far from my house.

I snuck up behind him and kicked him hard in the knee as he was fumbling around with his belt buckle. He went down like a sack of cement. The woman screamed mistaking me for a predator and started to hit me with a glass bottle. "Hey! I am trying to save your stupid ass. Now quit fucking hitting me and get the fuck out of here!" I screamed at her. The tattoos started to chant "Take her too! She hurts her kids! Take her too!" She kept hitting me, eventually screaming I hit her in the head. She slid down right on top of the man who had hit his head on the concrete. With ease, I picked them both up and carried them to my place.

I quickly chained them up with the chains that I brought with me from Cindy's house. I began to drain the man's blood into a huge bucket. Once the blood leaves the body he would be no match or would survive long. That didn't take long to do but right as every last drop had hit the bucket the woman woke up.

"What the fuck are you?" She shrieked. My fucking God was her voice annoying. She started sobbing which was louder than her voice. "Why are you doing this? You are so beautiful, you can have anything in the world! Why pick on me?" A snot bubble formed out of her nose and ran onto her lip. I ignored her while I grabbed another bucket. I started to drain her blood and then grabbed a chair to sit down in front of her. "Is that is important my beauty? To tell you the truth I am not just someone pretty. I am a man-made beast. You on the other hand are just a very bad person. Right now, I just need your soul." The color of her skin was starting to drain a little bit. "Why do you hurt your kids?" I asked digging the dirt out from under my nails. "How do you know that? Who told you?" She was shrieking. She was starting to get weaker so the shriek wasn't quite as shrill.

"Oh, so it is true then. You are a piece of shit. No kid EVER should be abused!" Her head was lolling around. I looked at the clock. I wasn't hungry but I was going to gorge on both of them within the next 48 hours. I had never had to eat two people at the same time before. She had a couple of minutes left until all the blood was drained from her body. The woman was bubbling and sobbing. Snot was dripping out of her nose and into her very wide mouth. I think she was praying or confessing it was all unintelligible nonsense.

Some sort of animalistic rage bubbled over inside of me and I started to punch her. It felt strange to punch someone, her skin almost felt rubbery because of the lack of blood. I couldn't stop punching her in the face. I was screaming at her as her bones were crunching loudly with each hit. I must have had hit her maybe a hundred times. Her face was unrecognizable and sunken in like it was made from bad jello. I couldn't tell when she had died but there were just enough brains left for me to eat. I checked the time. The man had already been dead for an hour, I was going to have to be quick.

The rest of the night went to chopping and grinding. I decided to grind both bodies together. There was not a lot of time to consume both bodies separately. I didn't see the harm in it. Then all I would need would be two more souls. I had memorized the entire ritual I would have to do in order to get to Mr. Rumple. All I needed were two more people. Two very bad people. I hurriedly ate without tasting the food. I spent until dawn eating. When I had consumed every last bit of it I spent a couple of hours cleaning.

Normally things were easier to clean but this was more than normal. I was exhausted and finally fell asleep around noon. My arm started to hurt as the tattoo began to form. I was too tired to move and did my best to sleep through the annoying jabbing I felt in my arm. I woke up it was well past midnight. I looked at the tattoo and gasped in horror. The faces of the two people I ate with the night before had merged together. Did that mean the souls were merged together? "Three more." The faces on my arm whispered. It did me no good to eat both of the bodies together. I still had three more to go. "FUCK!" I just wanted to be done with the carnage and eating people. I missed chocolate. I couldn't bear the smell of it anymore.

In three days, there was supposed to be a full lunar eclipse, that would be the best time to go grab Mr. Rumple from his hell. That didn't leave any time to make mistakes. I had just enough time to shower before I knew I had to go find my three souls. The night was the muggiest it had been. The air felt heavier than normal. "Miss!" A familiar voice sounded behind me. It was Matt walking up behind me."I'm sorry I can't sit for a picture. I have a lot to do and with no time." Matt smiled and it sent a shiver down my spine. "I can help." He offered his hand to me. "Sorry, I don't think you could help me with this one," I said sadly.

I couldn't tell him how badly I wanted to blow off the mission and just spend the evening with him. "Ah, you are going soul hunting huh?" He said quietly. I stepped back away from him trying hard not to show him my surprise. "I can help. I am assuming you need bad souls? I know of a place where you can find the worst sort of people. Just tell me what I need to do." He took a hold of my hand. The warmth surprised me. No human hand should ever be that warm. "Why are you wanting to help me?" I didn't trust him even though I wanted to. I jerked my hand away from his. The warmth was making my hand sweaty.

"Consider it my good deed for the year. I've been trying to earn some brownie points." He said quietly. "Why, what did you do?" I asked as I tied my hair up into a ponytail. "I pissed off my dad. Come on I'll show you the place." He tugged at my hand briefly and I jerked my hand away once more. "What do you get from helping me? I am not going to reward you." I knew I sounded harsh but if anything in this life has taught me anything it is to never trust anyone who says they will help you without naming a price."I just want to show my dad that I am very capable of being helpful." He started to walk down the bridge over the river that always looked murky no matter what time of the day it was.

I stood there for a few minutes debating on whether or not I should follow him. Sighing loudly, I began to run after him. I had given him quite the headstart and he was past the bridge. My lungs hurt and my calves were burning as I ran. I caught up with him panting and gasping for breath. He smiled and waited until I was able to continue. "What's your name by the way? I don't think you ever told it to me." He offered me a bottle of water from one of the vendors that were closing up their booth for the night. "Beauty," I said gulping the water. It was sweet and the best tasting water I had ever had in my life. Lying about my name had become second nature to me. All I had to do was see Cindy's face on my arm.

We were walking for a good hour when we came to a waterfall that I had never seen before. Matt grinned at me and dove right into the downward spray of water from the waterfall. I followed and was surprised to see it was a door. Matt opened the door and I could see a dimly lit hallway. He started to walk in and I closed the door firmly behind us. "How many souls do you need?" Matt had asked. There were so many steel doors along the hallway that I didn't hear him ask me anything. The air was chilly and I was starting to shiver. "Beauty, how many souls do you need?" Matt repeated himself this time louder. "I need 3. I have to consume their entire body one at a time." I said concentrating on the details on each steel door. "This is a secret prison run by the government. Behind each door is a prisoner who used to work for the government. They were highly experimented on. Some mutated to the point of no recognition. Some lost their minds and stare dumbly at the wall. Some of them became so violent that steel was not strong enough to hold them. Those will be the ones for you. We have to go to the bottom floor for those prisoners."

He pushed a small button on the side of one of the steel doors. A small elevator opened and we stepped in. "The best part is you can cook and eat them in their own rooms. You will be provided with everything you need, including a paralyzing agent if you need it. The ones on the bottom floor the government doesn't do much with. They get fed every four days hard bread that is starting to mold and river water. If three of them come up missing, the government won't bat an eye. My sister runs the place she gave me access to make sure no one escapes. I am sure she won't mind if I bring you."

On the bottom floor, there were four huge doors. The doors had carvings on them that looked like ancient warnings and were made from a material I didn't recognize. "If you would like to cut back on some time I can start two pressure cookers for you. I'll make sure

I include everything." I nodded. I was too nervous to concentrate. Matt handed me a small backpack with everything I would need to take out the first prisoner.

I was expecting a behemoth of a man standing there in chains. What I saw was a thin man who was chewing on a mangled piece of steel shelf. He had long white hair and a white beard to match. His teeth were all jagged and bleeding. His hands were gnarled into horrible shapes from what looked like to be from arthritis. I looked back at Matt. "Don't let his appearance fool you. He used to lure women and kids with an ice cream truck then do unspeakable horrible things to them." He pointed to the guy. I stuck him in the arm with the paralyzing agent and watched his body go limp. He smelled horrible. Out of the corner of my eye, I saw Matt start dropping body parts into two pressure cookers true to his word. Sighing heavily, I took a bite out of the man's arm. His skin tasted like it hadn't been washed in decades. Matt offered some sort of sauce to pour on the man. The sauce helped a little bit, at least it masked the man's stench.

I couldn't decide which body made me the sickest to eat, Cindy's decaying body or this man. I closed my eyes and just kept taking huge bites. Most of the time I was able to swallow the flesh whole without doing a lot of chewing. It took me four hours to completely devour the man. The tattoo started to form on my arm while I began to eat out of one of the pressure cookers. I could hardly tell I was eating a human being at all. It was seasoned greatly even the eyeballs. Because it was so good, that body had only taken me a couple of hours to eat. By the time I got to the third body, I had to rest. My stomach was distended and was hurting to the point where sweat poured down my body.

Matt sat down with me as I let my stomach settle for a little while. Before I knew it, we were talking and laughing up a storm. He was so easy to talk to. I didn't tell him anything about my past, instead, we shared stories of the idiot people we had come across in our lives. I didn't want the night to end but I still had one more body to eat. I quickly started to eat out of the pressure cooker. The meat was hot and practically melted in my mouth. I finished a little bit before dawn and the last tattoo started to form on my arm.

I tried to stand but because I was sitting for so long my legs didn't want to move. "Hey let's just grab this room and get some sleep," Matt said offering pillows and blankets. I didn't want to put myself at risk but was too tired. I let Matt carry me to bed and snuggle up with me in his arms. I fell asleep listening to his heartbeat on his chest. I hadn't been held in so long, I had forgotten how much I missed it. Almost instantly, I was asleep.

When I woke up I was chained to the bed. Matt was standing beside a tall beautiful woman. Everything felt blurry and out of focus as I tried to open my eyes. "Sorry about the effects. They do wear off. I couldn't take the risk of you waking up too soon." Matt said from across the room. "What's going on?" I already guessed that I shouldn't have trusted Matt. "You're my ticket home. I want you to meet my sister, Goldie." Matt said as both of them moved closer to the bed. Goldie? Where had I heard that name before? My head was spinning and I felt dizzy.

"Hello, Beauty," Goldie said as she leaned down to where we were face to face. She had a weird glow around her that made my eyes water. "I understand that my idiot brother is trying to help you. What's your mission? Why do you need that many souls?" Goldie moved a piece of hair from my forehead. "I have a mission and I can't fail. I have to take down a corporation that experimented on me and killed my friend." "How do you plan on doing that?" Goldie said as she gave me a sip of water through a straw. Suddenly, it hit me. Goldie was Mr. Rumple's daughter. He was dragged to hell by his daughter and her mother to be tortured for all eternity.

"Goldie, I have to get Mr. Rumple to stop The MEC. They are experimenting with people. They almost killed me. They have killed thousands." I was being honest because I knew Goldie would kill me with a slice of a finger if I lied. "I can't let you do that Beauty. He can't return." Goldie unlocked the chains and let me sit up. "I know all the terrible things he has done. I have to resurrect him because he is the only one who can stop The MEC." I was trying to sound tough but I knew this was going to be a hard sale to win. Goldie sat down beside me. "I understand, The MEC is on the list for Hell. However, you will have to speak to someone first. Releasing Mr. Rumple is a very bad idea." Goldie pulled me up. "Wait. I know I have to go to Hell to talk to this person. I have to cover up one soul. She was the friend who sacrificed herself for me. Her soul is not a bargain." Goldie nodded. "Which one?" She asked peering at my arm. I put my hand over Cindy's face. "This one." Goldie nodded and touched Cindy's face. "It will be covered as long as you are in Hell. Once you are back on this plane, her face will reappear."

"It's time to go home, Matt." Goldie touched the wall beside the bed and flames licked it. The flames looked like ancient runes and another door formed. The heat was severe and instantly felt like I had stepped into a pressure cooker. Goldie took me by the arm and my tattoos were shining bright. Surprisingly, the heat didn't hurt me as we walked. We didn't walk long before we came to a throne that was made from skulls. A man sat there playing on a cellphone a game that looked like candy crush.

"Goldie you've returned. I see you have brought your useless brother. Why?" The man asked in a deep distorted tone. He had a strange glow around him making all his facial features look like glass. "He found Beauty." She said as she pushed me forward. She showed him my arm with the tattoos. "Goodness, that's a good amount of souls. Tell me what are you going to do with all those souls?" He put away the cellphone and focused his attention on me. "Hello, sir. I need to exchange these souls for Mr. Rumple to take down The MEC." I was trying my best to not sound nervous.
"No way." He sounded irritated. "You couldn't handle Mr. Rumple and there is no way I can release the creation I made onto the physical plane ever again." I could see Matt cowering beside me. "Get out of my face and take Matt with you." He shooed me away like I was a fly.

"Let me prove to you that I can handle the task of making sure Mr. Rumple doesn't hurt anyone but The MEC." I hadn't realized that I was bowing to the man. Blood was forming from under my knee as the hard, hot rocks dug deep. "Ok, I am interested. Let's see what you got Beauty. Bring him out. Make yourself fucking useful Matt."

Matt nodded and hurried away. He looked like he was about to cry. I rolled my eyes. "What's the deal between you two?" I asked. I was still kneeling but I wasn't afraid. "He is always fucking things up. Can't handle the simplest tasks." He sighed tiredly. "Big deal. You should have had my childhood." I didn't lower my eyes and kept him in eye contact with me. He leaned forward to see into my eyes. "Yes, I can see that. Nonetheless, your past made you stronger. His past, makes him cry on a nightly basis." His distorted voice that was close to my face made blood slowly slide out of my eyes.

I lowered my voice and kept staring into his glass-like eyes. "I was made stronger because people of The MEC experimented on me. I have never met a nice human being that hadn't hurt me in some stupid way. I will give up my soul, just for the chance to take The MEC down. I will give you each of their souls on a fucking platter." He leaned closer and whispered, "Why would I accept your offer when I can collect all those souls on my own?" I didn't care that my eyes were starting to burn and I could feel more blood slide down my cheeks. "If I do it, it gives you more time to play candy crush." I laughed. For a second he said nothing, but then he joined in laughing. More blood was now dripping out of my ears. Matt returned holding a man by chains that were made from a sort of weird fire. I could tell he used to be quite handsome but was not much to look at now.

The man sitting on the throne clapped his hands loudly. "Mr. Rumple. This girl right here wants you to kill thousands of people who work for a company that experimented on her." I stood up from the rocks and faced Mr. Rumple. Mr. Rumple started to speak. "Let's make a deal." His voice sounded raspy, probably from all the screaming he had done. Matt took off his chains and let Mr. Rumple get closer to me. "I don't make deals with bad guys."

I said standing up straight. I saw Matt's jaw drop and the man on the throne moved closer to me. "You will do exactly as I say when I say it. I will not make a single deal with you. You are transferring prisons and I will be your warden." Mr. Rumple leaned down to look me in the face. Before he could say anything he hit me square in the chest. "You better learn how to talk to people. I will do no such thing." He whispered and threw another punch into my ribs. I stood up and smiled. I remembered what Cindy had said about embracing what I was capable of.

I could feel a different heat radiating from my body. Every single rock around me stood up around me as I took a painful deep breath. I let him hit me one more time so he could get closer. I moved the floating rocks to build a tight circle around us. "You won't be making any deals. Your job is to destroy The MEC. That is all." I said to him. The faces on my arm felt alive and made it feel like my arm was being caught in an electric fence. I grabbed Mr.Rumple and used my tattooed arm to dig into his chest. The faces seemed to be helping chew through the flesh as I dug deeper inside. I grabbed his heart and ripped it clean out of his chest. The hot spray of bone and blood splashed me in the face. His blood was burning my face, but I didn't feel it. I smiled once more at him before I shoved his burning heart into my mouth. It had a nice crispy outer shell and tasted like bacon. I could hear Matt throwing up in the corner and Goldie gasping. The man stood up from the throne and pushed Mr. Rumple out of the way. I felt amazing and could see every vein in my body light up through my pale skin as if it was the fire.

"I see I won't have to worry about Mr. Rumple causing any harm. You, my dear, are very dangerous. You can have him. Once you get your revenge, my dear, there will be a seat right here waiting for you." He smiled and dropped all the rocks that were floating around me. "I just want to be cured. I just want to go back as Joannie, not Beauty and not this Beast." I whispered. The bleeding had stopped coming from my ears and eyes. "I'm afraid that will no longer be possible. You ate a heart out of Hell. This means, you now will belong to Hell. No matter how much good you try to do, you will end up here. You may as well embrace your gifts. You may as well have a seat with the royal family. Rather than being torn to shreds." His face finally came into focus.

He looked amazing even though he looked like he was made from fiery glass. "I want to be able to have a life and when I die then I will come to Hell." I ran my finger across his cheek and watched him closely as I licked the blood from my finger. It kept bleeding a little bit and I offered it to the man. He smiled and licked my blood until it had stopped bleeding. It looked completely healed but scarred. "I find you quite refreshing." He said distortedly. "You have a deal."

Another woman came up and smiled at me. "You must be Mallory, Goldie's mother," I whispered. I bowed to her as well. "You are correct. There's no way I'm allowing him to be taken back to the living, without some sort of insurance policy." Mallory leaned down and whispered something into the ear of the man. The man nodded. He stood up and called Matt over to him. "You are still on probation. So your mother and I have come to an agreement. You will also go back. You will make sure Mr.Rumple does only what Beauty says. He must not make any sort of deals with anyone, nor is he allowed to kill anyone that is not The MEC. If you do this correctly without messing up, you will be allowed back at the table. All your past fuckups will be forgiven." The man grabbed Matt and shoved him inside of Mr.Rumple without waiting for Matt to say a word.

"You will only address him from now on as Mr. Rumple. He has to pay for what he has done in the past. If you mention the name Matt, your death will be short and you won't be taking The MEC down. Mr. Rumple will only have the powers to do anything that you tell him to do. If you order him to hurt anyone that is not connected to The MEC, he will defy that order and will be the cause of your death. Do you understand Beauty?" The man said distorted. "Yes, sir I understand. I will not let you down." I said making sure I didn't keep my eyes off of him.

Goldie and Mallory hugged me tightly. Their body heat made my body sweat. It was strange that in Hell the heat didn't make me sweat. "Thank you," I whispered to them. Goldie and Mallory left from the same exit that Mr. Rumple had used earlier. "Oh and Beauty? One last thing." He grabbed me by arm and took all the souls from it except for Cindy's. He took each soul and slurped it loudly into his mouth. Then he spit into his hand a ruby. The ruby was aflame and I could hear screaming coming from inside. He shoved it deep into where Mr.Rumple's heart once was. My arm felt naked without all the tattoos. Then he grabbed me close to him and kissed me so deeply that my legs felt weak. I didn't care that my lips were bleeding. The kiss was the most amazing kiss I had ever had. He grabbed my wrist and burned a symbol onto it. "You will belong to me." He whispered to me. "What about Mallory?" I couldn't catch my breath. "You will be my queen." He lifted up my chin. His eyes were bottomless and dark green.

"Queen? I don't think I have the heart for it." I whispered sadly. Mr. Rumple laughed. "What do you mean Beauty?" He kissed me again. "How can I be a queen of Hell if I am not a bad person?" I hated how whiny I sounded. "This isn't really Hell Beauty. This is the place right before you reach Hell. I am not the devil. My name is Dilan and I landed here a very long time ago. I accidentally created the first Mr. Rumple. There have been many Mr. Rumples but this one here was the evilest of them all. I struck a deal with the real devil to hold him here."

"So, what would I be the queen of? A fiery room?" I couldn't help but ask. None of it made sense to me. "My dear Beauty, this room is temporary. Once you return Mr.Rumple, he will go to Hell. I will leave. Goldie and Mallory have decided to ascend back to the living as reincarnated souls as their reward. You will come with me. I think it's time I went home. You will rule with me." He smiled. I didn't know what to say to any of that. It sounded farfetched. Mr. Rumple came up behind me as I was looking into Dilan's eyes.

Mr. Rumple bit me hard on the neck. I could feel blood pouring down my shoulder and I felt weakened. I could hear Dilan roar something just as everything went fuzzy. I could taste something bitter slide down my throat. It felt like fire and burned all the way through my body. Things became clearer and I could see that I had slipped back down on the rocks. Mr. Rumple and Dilan were fighting. I touched my throat and realized I had completely healed. I stood up and screamed until both men stopped hitting each other. "ENOUGH! Now, I don't know what in the hell is going on here. I don't care right now. I need to get The MEC now!" I realized I was screaming and both men had their hands over their ears. I had caused both of them to bleed out of their ears as mine had done.

Mr. Rumple smiled. "I guess we will see which man she will pick after the end of everything." He smirked at Dilan. "That will teach you not to treat your son like you have. We both have marked her now." Dilan looked like he was going to say something.

"What have you done?" He whispered as he looked at me. Mr. Rumple had gone silent as well. "I am not a consolidation prize," I said. "We can discuss this later. I am running out of time. I need to go now." I grabbed Mr.Rumple by the arm and started to head to the door. "What are you now?" Mr. Rumple whispered. I chose not to answer him. Dilan opened the door. "Be careful Beauty."

I looked back at Dilan to see the concern on his face. "It's not me you have to worry about," I said to him as I firmly closed the door. As soon as we stepped outside I could hear Mr. Rumple groaning. I watched as his body began to regrow the muscles that had long since burned off. He looked like he had no skin for the longest time as the blood vessels regrew onto his body. The blood vessels attached themselves to the ruby with the souls in it. I waited impatiently as Mr. Rumple continued to groan loudly as his body reformed. The skin was next it seemed to take the longest as it stretched all around his body before forming tightly across everything else. His teeth formed which dropped him down to his knees. Then his hair and finally his suit appeared. When Allisha McAdoo had first written Rumply Chronicles, she had described him as a blonde with dark green eyes. This Mr. Rumple now had jet black hair with a dark red streak in it. He still had green eyes but now had a golden ring around the pupil. He was taller like Matt had been. When he finally stood up, he adjusted his expensive cuff links and smoothed out the wrinkles of his silk suit. "Are you done?" I asked impatiently. He nodded and began to follow me. I checked my cell phone to my dismay I had lost a week and a half getting Mr. Rumple. Time was becoming my enemy.

I had to relocate Isaac's location. I blasted the ac on full blast and started the long drive back to Kansas. Isaac had moved a few miles away from where Mr. Rumple had died not so long ago. "We are going back close to your hometown," I smirked as I stepped on the gas. I didn't care that I was speeding, for the first time in my life I felt alive. I felt like I finally had a purpose and it wasn't to be abused. I was happy to go back to Kansas, Florida's heat was insufferable. Mr. Rumple stared at me in silence the entire drive. Ignoring him, and not slowing down I cranked up the music.

I eventually stopped to get some rest. I didn't really feel like I needed to sleep I guess it was just out of habit. As soon as I found a hotel it started to downpour. The rain pelted me hard like it was an angry toddler. The lady at the check-in counter barely looked at me. She was busy flirting with some sort of skater boy who looked like he didn't finish high school. I snuck behind the counter and grabbed myself a key. The room was subpar at best and a gigantic roach flittered across the floor. I rolled my eyes. "Quit staring at me!" I hissed at him. I went to the bathroom and looked at myself in the mirror. My eyes had changed colors. They looked like red crystals. Cindy's face was back on my arm but the entire arm was now covered in shimmering splinters. My veins were black and looked like crooked highways all over my body. I looked scary. I felt amazing. I wanted to give myself a makeover something edgier. My hair looked longer and had a dark blood-red streak. Mr. Rumple was sitting on the bed looking bored when I reentered the room. The shower although it was quick seemed to help me feel more like me again.

"So why did you bite me?" I asked as I towel-dried my hair slowly. I had already been marked by Dilan so it didn't make sense to me for Mr. Rumple to do something like that. "I wanted you for my own. Dilan is a parasite, he doesn't deserve someone like you." I rolled my eyes. "Let me guess, someone as beautiful as me really belongs with someone like you right? Let me fill in on a secret. I hate life. I hate people. There is no one who is a decent person. Cindy was, but this world ate her, well rather I had to. Whether I belong to Dilan, or to you, it doesn't matter. I am going to take down The MEC, then I get to die. Fuck this life and everyone else in it. Dilan's mark is just a scar, you biting me is just another scar as well. Nothing means anything to me. I lost so many fucking years being a human guinea pig. All for money. All because I hated my life, I wanted to get the fuck off the streets. Then The MEC made me want to give up. Cindy saved my life over and over again. She and my hallucinations kept telling me to survive. I know my only purpose in this dreadful life is to take down The MEC. So don't get it twisted, there's nothing left for me after this task. Love doesn't exist, happiness doesn't exist, all that matters is making sure they don't make anyone else like me." I tossed the towel back into the bathroom.

"I can understand that, I really do. My entire life once I became Mr. Rumple was all about the next deal. I loved Mallory very much, she was my best friend as you probably read in Rumple Chronicles. In the end, my own evilness took over. Goldie and Mallory will always hate me." I stopped him right before he could say anymore. "I don't pity you. I won't. Your sob story is justifyingly your own fault. Just as mine is. If I hadn't signed up for the experiment, I would not be alive today. We aren't going to be bonding. What happened to the author who knew everything about you?" I began to braid my hair.

"Fine, why don't we use this time to find Isaac's location?" "I already do. We leave in an hour." I said as I began to count down the second in my head. Alice was bouncing around the room laughing loudly. "Shut up!" I hissed at her. I gave myself the injection to curb the side effects that Cindy had left for me. Mr. Rumple watched me closely. "Allisha McAdoo is still out there, no doubt started writing again. It used to irk me so much that she knew everything about me and I didn't know a thing about her. She was in my thoughts a lot while I was being tortured."

"Well if she's lucky, she'll stick to the shadows then. I would hate for you to disobey me." I smirked. It was finally time to go. "Let's go. You will make sure all the patients will be sent to real hospitals with their files. They will need proper care. All the dead, those files will be given to the proper authorities." Mr. Rumple cut me off. "Authorities don't care about medical experiments. Why would they care about the dead? The dead were fed to other patients."

"That means they probably won't get those patients' help or even lock up the doctors. Especially in today's world. Everything gets so twisted, riots happen, and cops are no longer protecting anyone because they fear death from some sort of Karen. Everything today is all about scandals, viruses, and which country has the biggest resources." I knew I was thinking out loud. "I guess it's just up to me then. I'll kill them all. All the patients and the Drs." I grabbed my car keys and phone and then started to head out to the car once more. "Wait, wait, wait, did you just say you're going to kill the patients too? How will that help them? Wouldn't that make you as bad as Isaac?" Mr. Rumple hurriedly got into the car and strapped in his seatbelt. "I'm going to kill the patients for the simple fact, that if I allow them to live who knows how they will have to be a weapon. If not for Isaac then the government. One person who has been experimented on is all it takes. Suddenly, world war three is to our advantage. Those people don't deserve that. They have been through enough." I said once more speeding towards my destination. The car was going over 90 mph and it still felt like it was barely moving.

"What do you need me for?" Mr.Rumple asked breaking me out of the trance I had fallen into. "Aren't you the muscle?" I asked. "Oh is it because you were merged with you know who? Is that why you're asking me all this crap? Goldie's brother, I am sure was a nice guy and all but don't be going all soft on me. I don't need a whiny overpriced toddler who can't handle his job." I glared at him. "You're the boss." He said looking at me. My arm that had the crystal shards was starting to throb. For a second, I saw nothing but red. Taking a deep breath, I calmed myself down for when I saw Isaac. I would never admit out loud that I was looking for to this day for so long.

I recognized Cindy's brother almost immediately when I pulled up. This MEC looked different than the one I went to. This one was red and black. He nodded and let me in without saying a word to me. He eyed Mr.Rumple until it looked like he couldn't move his neck anymore. "This place is heavily armed. We need to find Isaac's office. You take the hallway to the left, I will take the hallway to the right. If they are wearing white coats kill them and bring me their hearts. If they are wearing black scrubs, those are surgeons, kill them and bring me their brains. If they are wearing blue scrubs and look terrified in their eyes, they probably are the good ones. Just bring them to me alive, but tape up their hands and feet. All patients, give them all a dangerously high dosage of whatever will kill them in their sleep. They have suffered enough. If anyone tries to hurt you or get to me, kill them and bring me their heads ripped off their body. There are duffle bags in the locker rooms. Now go! If you find Isaac bring him to me." I growled. I could see he was torn in what I was saying to him. I slapped him hard across the face with the hand that had crystal shards in it. It cut him deep on the cheek. "Pay attention to what I told you, or I will make your life a living hell to the point where you'll be begging to go back to Dilan!" My veins were blackish red and throbbing to the point where they looked like they were moving out of the skin.

I didn't let Mr.Rumple argue with me. I took off running on the right. The first person I saw was wearing black scrubs. My stomach grumbled loudly. I used my crystalized arm and hit him hard enough to drop him to the floor. I took his hair and ripped it all the way back until I could see nothing more but a bloody skull with pieces of ripped flesh on it. I shoved my hand deep into his skull and scooped out his brain. I ripped it off of the spine and started to shove pieces of it into my mouth. It was slimy but I was so hungry I didn't care. I started using the broken skull as a spoon to make sure I got every piece of the brain. His legs were still twitching as I left him.

The first door was of a patient so I quietly snuck in. I saw the man was sleeping so I grabbed all the syringes I could find and stuck them all into his arm until his heart exploded out of his chest. I was about to leave the room when I decided, I was still hungry. I grabbed the pieces of the man's heart and shoved them into my mouth as I continued down the hallway. Four brains, seven hearts, and 22 patients later I finally found Isaac. He was busy getting a blow job from a nurse that was naked. She had deep gashed scars running all down her back and legs. "You need to leave before I kill you too," I said loudly, wiping the blood away from my mouth. The woman jumped and bit down hard on Isaac's dick. He shoved her to the floor and I could see blood trickling down the shaft. "Hello, Dr. Isaac Hyde," I said smiling. The woman was scrambling around trying to find her clothes. She had no eyes just empty sockets. I handed her the clothes on the floor and directed her towards the door.

"Surprise!" I said laughing. Isaac wasn't paying attention to me he was trying to stop the slight bleeding from his dick with a piece of tissue. It irritated me. I could feel the heat coming from my eyes. I could see the heat coming from my body as I charged over to Isaac. I pushed him down onto the seat he had been sitting in and grabbed a hold of his limp dick in my hand. I started to stroke it until it was nice and hard. His head was tilted back and his eyes closed so he didn't notice when I put my mouth on it until I started to suck. He let out a groan just as I started to bite through the flesh of his shaft. He was screaming and squirming around until I bit completely through the shaft.

I spit out the pitiful dick into my hand and grabbed Isaac's jaw. I ripped his jaw off completely with my crystal arm then shoved his own dick into his mouth until there wasn't anything but severed tissue sticking up from the back of his throat. He was gagging and gurgling as he tried to get his dick out of his throat. I grabbed each finger and bent them into unnatural angles until they snapped. Gray bones were poking out all over his fingers. "I think first, I will take your eyes," I whispered to him.

I poked my fingernail into his eye just in the corner. Then I started to use my fingernail to saw through the optical nerve until the eyeball plopped into my hand. I shoved it into my mouth and crunched down on it until the eyeball itself popped all over Isaac's face. I did the same thing to his other eyeball. He was still making that strangling sound as he tried to breathe. I had never been so hungry in my entire life. I cut his chest with my fingernails that had suddenly grown into sharp talons. I pulled apart his ribcage until his heart was exposed. I didn't bother to take it out of his body before I started to chew through it. It was bitter but it didn't stop me from eating the entire thing. I took one of his ribs and bent it back to make myself a makeshift knife.

I started to saw through his skull. I ate his brain without breathing much. After I was done, I had to stop for a few minutes to catch my breath. I shoved the lifeless body out of the chair and sat down. It had already had tabs open to each patient and the money they were earning. Each patient had no other family or friends. I took all the money and transferred it all to my account. I had no intentions of keeping any of the money, before my death I had planned to help up the people who ended up as I did on the streets.

It was time to see what Mr.Rumple turned up. I slowly made my way to the main lobby before slowly making my way to the left hallway. After all the body parts I had eaten in the last hour, I was still beyond hungry. I found Mr. Rumple in the last room. All the patients had been euthanized according to my wishes. In each arm, there were dozens of syringes. Some of their hearts exploded, some of their eyes and brains exploded. I ate everything that was outside the bodies. There was one nurse who was quietly sobbing and was taped up. I went down on my knees and looked at her deeply. "You are a good soul. It's not your fault. You get to live today. I am going to remove the tape from your mouth ok?" I said. She looked scared of me but nodded slightly. She was missing her mouth and part of her cheek. "I want you to do something for me ok? I am going to transfer some money to you and I want you to find everyone who is living off of the streets within the state. If they aren't booze hounds or druggies, I want you to give them some money. Enough to get themselves a place and live until they can find a place of employment. I will give you a special gift since you can not speak. With this gift, you will be able to see the poor souls who were like me. Those who are just unfortunate as I was, will have a blue glow around them. Those who are con artists, bad people, or addicted to some sort of substance, will have a black glow around them. Will you do this for me?" I asked her as I wiped her tears from her face with a tissue. She looked at me and took a deep breath. "I am a result of being experimented on by Isaac Hyde. He will no longer be a bother to you. No one who did anything bad at The MEC will ever harm you or anyone else again. Will you do this for me?" I asked her again. She nodded.

I cut off the tape on her wrists and ankles. She wrote down her account number. "I will give you enough for you as well to use as you see fit. The money may as well go for a good cause. The patients won't be needing it. No one should have to go through anything that they have." She nodded and gave me a small hug. I could tell she wanted to smile. I transferred money over to her. "I plan on taking down all The MECs in the world. Each one like you will be given the same task." I whispered. I was about to leave the room when she signaled me to wait a second. She started to type on the computer and printed out a few pages. She handed me the pages. The pages contained where each MEC was located, who the main doctor was, how many patients, and how much security. I gave her a hug. "You must leave this place and never look back. Take the doorman with you. He is an old friend of mine." I wrote down that Cindy's soul is safe and The MECs were going down. I wrote that if he wanted to he could help out the woman standing in front of me. I looked at her nametag. She had the same name as my mother. I looked at her closer. She wasn't my mother but I had to be sure. I gave her the note. Then with my crystalized hand, I gently touched her eyes. "My gift to you," I whispered to her. Her eyes started to water but then took on a greenish hue to them. "Don't worry about the blood. Just go out the front door and take the doorman with you. Thank you for your help." I whispered to her. She gave me another hug and practically ran for the front door.

In the last room, Mr. Rumple had gathered everyone else. I growled at them all even though they were all dead. He had lined them up nicely along the wall. I began to eat to my heart's content until each one was just a bloody congealed mess of meat. I stood up covered from head to toe in blood, flesh, and guts. "Now it's time to burn this fucking place to Hell." As I made my way to the door, Mr. Rumple grabbed my arm and pulled me close to him. He kissed me so deeply that I almost forgot I was covered in massacred body parts. "I will go to the ends of the Earth and back for you." He whispered against my lips. It had been so long since I had felt a compassionate touch. Without thinking about what I was doing, I tackled Mr. Rumple to the floor. We had ripped off each other's clothes in such a frenzy right in the middle of the dead bodies. Sex had never been a thing for me, but I couldn't believe how much I had wanted it.

We had the roughest sex ever until neither of us could breathe. We lay in the body heap gasping for breath. For the first time in my life, I had been satisfied. I had never thought sex would feel so amazing before. My clothes were ripped to shreds so I went through other people's bags until I found some clothes that would fit me. I took a quick shower to wash all the blood off of my body as Mr. Rumple watched me with a smile on his face. He was in the shower adjacent to mine but had scrubbed so quickly that he was just standing there watching me. I quickly got dressed in a mini skirt and tank top. I even found some makeup and carefully put a little bit on. I looked at the mirror then at Mr. Rumple who was smiling at me. For once in my life, I didn't hate myself so much to be covered. I had never dressed provocatively before. I had always hated everything about myself.

"One last thing before we burn this fucker to the ground. We have to find the room where they ground up the dead into steaks. I'll go find it, you make sure you wipe every single thing from every computer. Be sure to take every piece of paper and put it in the middle. All that shit has to be burnt." I said as I brushed out my hair and braided it once more. Mr. Rumple quickly got dressed in another expensive suit that made him look dashing. I hurried to the basement and gasped at what I saw. Dead bodies were kept in tanks that were filled with millions of maggots and leeches. They had already been cut up into steaks that were kept in a freezer.

Flies buzzed all around the place and the amount of sticky blood was enough to make me gag. I pushed the intercom button and said, "Mr. Rumple please bring all paperwork and computers to the basement. Be quick about it!" I snapped. I ran back to Isaac's office. I grabbed all the jars of eyeballs I could find. There were so many of them. I found an old dumb waiter that led directly to the basement so, after about twelve times, I had most of the jars in the basement as well. I kept about five of the jars for myself as a snack.

I met Mr. Rumple back in the basement as he was pouring gasoline on everything. I opened the freezer door so we could burn the meat inside of it as well. I couldn't find any matches. I used my arm with the crystal shards to start a massive fire. I felt my veins on fire as Mr. Rumple and I ran out of the building holding hands. I made sure my crystalized arm hit every wall I could before we reached outside.

The wind had picked up and whipped around us. Mr. Rumple got into the car and I stood there watching the fire lick the entire building like a child with an ice cream cone. The flames shot up and looked like it almost hit the sky as the building began to collapse on itself.
I jumped into the car and we started to speed away. For a long time, Mr.Rumple didn't say a word to me. I listened to music as loud as my ears could handle. For the first time since he left his prison tomb, he wasn't staring at me.

We moved on to the next location. It was smaller than the one Isaac had managed so it didn't take quite as long. I was being fed, and I managed to save at least two people in each building. The news was picked up on all the buildings burning. They were calling it an act of terrorism. Anything they didn't want people to know about, the cover story was always the same. Terrorism. I was beginning to enjoy my mission. Each one was almost as like the first one I did. I lost track of how many people I ate, I stopped the injections that Cindy had left behind for me. I was able to embrace all my powers. I was getting creative with all the doctors in each MEC. Some died like Isaac, others were beaten with their own dick while their balls were shoved into their mouths. The women doctors I usually would gut them enough to get their intestines and then strangle them with their intestines. I was enjoying watching the life dim from their eyes.

I should have remembered that with anything that comes with enjoyment for me comes something hellish in return. I had just finished the last MEC on the list. I didn't want to stop doing what I had been doing for the past four years. I enjoyed the carnage, the fires, the sex, and even was beginning to enjoy Mr. Rumple. He never judged me and became my best friend. I never liked the label friends with benefits so we decided to date.

It was on one of those dates that we ran into a problem. We had killed almost 89% of all doctors around the world. What doctors were left refused to practice medicine. The cops no longer patrolled the streets. The riots got worse when the government released yet another virus upon the world. People were becoming disfigured if they went outside to breathe. The very air became acid-like. The water in the oceans, lakes, and rivers turned black. People stopped working and began to blockade themselves in their houses. No one cared about their lawns so it was hard to tell where streets started and houses began.

Finding evil people was getting hard, and I was starving. I was so hungry I was extremely pissed off. Everything just stopped. The stores were empty. The government covered everything up that I had done to The MECs. They blamed it on other countries and before I knew it, life on Earth was a desolate wasteland consumed with hatred. Even those who braved the outside to try for supplies didn't satisfy me. Their bodies were filled with nasty, slimy, pus that was black. They smelled of burnt motor oil and toxic gas.

"I love you my beastly Beauty." Mr. Rumple murmured coming up behind me as I watched another fire break out from a riot. "I am fucking hungry! I'm about to fucking eat you!!" I screamed at him. I was so hungry and angry I didn't want to hear nice loving things. "I have an idea that will help us both out." He whispered in my ear. I bit him on the neck hard enough to get a small taste of blood. "Tell me before you become my dinner!" He grabbed my wrists and held me at arm's length away from him. "We are going to trick Dilan. He can fix this world, then you can eat him. I won't go back to that prison. We can stay here together." He pulled me closer to him and kissed me. "That won't work. He will see that coming." I whispered against his chest.

"All you have to do is say his son's name. His soul doesn't really exist inside me now. It seems that both of us are so madly in love with you, that he no longer cares about sitting with the royal family. Do the last ritual to send Cindy off to a better place, then let's do this together. Together, our love can outpower Dilan. Goldie and Mallory have already left to be reincarnated."

I thought about it. "What will I eat in the meantime?" I asked as my stomach growled like a beast loudly. "We can start breaking into people's houses and eating what's left." He laughed. I rolled my eyes. "What a fucking stupid ass idea." "Don't worry my love, I will provide you a meal. Go get ready for the ritual. The quicker we can get Dilan here, the faster our lives return to normal." I groaned again. "Fine!" I rolled my eyes. Mr. Rumple went to the freezer and pulled out a nice steak for me. Our provisions were running low. The last dead guy I killed to eat, I had to portion.

I had memorized the ritual and started to burn white candles in a circle. I grabbed a knife and delicately sliced off Cindy's face. I put it in the middle of the white candles. I didn't have any real flowers and I prayed the fake flowers I had found would suffice. "Thank you Cindy for all your help," I whispered to my skin that was staring at me. I could feel a tear sliding down my face and dripping onto my skin. I realized it was a drop of blood and not a tear. I gently wiped it off my skin and began to chant the chant I needed to.

"Blessed spirit it's time to be free
Unbind yourself from me
Go onto the heavens above
Fly with the white wings of a dove
Thank you for your help to me
It's time I set you free
Be free
My beautiful Cindy"

I kept chanting it over and over again trying to picture her kind eyes. My memory was still sharp as it had been all those years ago. I could see a beautiful white dove fly from the fake flowers. I watched as the dove burst into a water bubble. For a second, I could see Cindy smiling. Then all the candles burnt out all at once. I picked up each one wrapped it all with white ribbons and buried it deep in the backyard.

"It's done," I told Mr. Rumple as I pulled him close to me. I kissed him deeply and then put both of my hands on his face. He no longer minded when my crystal shards would cut his skin. He would usually heal pretty quickly and be even more stunning than before. "You ready for this Beauty?" He asked as he held out his hand to me. "I'm ready." I smiled. I could feel my eyes glowing out of my head.

Mr. Rumple and I started to dance with each other, our movements like unified liquid. "Matt!" I shouted then smiled as Mr. Rumple dipped me in for a twirl. The walls opened up and the fiery runes reappeared. Dilan appeared. "I told you what would happen if you uttered his name!" Dilan growled. He looked around and saw outside. "What in the fuck did you do Beauty!?" He screamed. Mr. Rumple and I kept dancing. Dilan cut his hands with a knife he had under his skull robe. As his blood hit the floor, life on Earth stopped still. Slowly like someone was pushing the rewind button on an old cassette tape everything started to go backward. The only ones not affected were Mr. Rumple and me. We continued to dance.

Mr. Rumple winked at me when Dilan's back was turned. Time to get rid of that parasite once and for all. I let Mr. Rumple toss me in the air and while his hands were up to catch me, I lept towards Dilan. I used my crystalized arm to grab him around his neck as I began to chew threw his throat. His blood tasted of moldy cheese and maggot guts. I wasn't going to let that stop me. I kept eating away until his head was entirely off his body. I stomped on his arms and legs to smash them into a million pieces. With each shard of crystal that fell onto the ground, I stuck it into my arm. At first, it stung a little bit but after doing that about fifty times, my arm became numb. Mr. Rumple hit Dilan in the torso with a sledgehammer that we had carefully hidden.

I ate all of his organs without bothering to cook any of them. They also tasted putrid. All I could do was close my eyes and shove the pieces in my mouth as quickly as I had done when I had to eat Cindy. Each piece of crystal even if it was a tiny grain I shoved into my arm. All that was left was his head. My entire arm was so full of crystal that I could hardly move it. It was bleeding and my veins were taking on a greenish-black hue all across my body.

"What have you done, you Beast?" Dilan asked as his

eyes rolled loosely around in his head. "Welcome to my Kingdom," I whispered as I smashed his face with my fist. I ate his eyes cutting up my tongue. They tasted of nothing, I hardly tasted the blood. I could see his brain oozing out of his cracked skull. It was full of millions of parasites. Dark purple worms wriggled in and out of each fold of the brain. I grabbed the brain while Mr. Rumple continued to shove pieces of crystal into my arm. In order for this to work, I had to make sure that every part of Dilan was a part of me. Each shard made a squishing sound but I hardly heard any of it as I stared at the brain.

I picked up the brain and could see the worms eating as they wriggled. I picked up one of the parasites to see it was made from nothing but teeth. When the last piece of crystal was shoved deep into my arm, it started to glow. "Bottoms up," I said eyeing the brain. This was going to suck. I shoved big bites of the brain, worms, and all into my mouth. I did my best to chew quickly but kept gagging. It was like eating a sandwich that had been stuck inside a dead body for a decade. In the end, I decided not to chew it. I would just swallow it all in small bites. I could feel the worms eating their way down to my stomach.

I could feel the worms wriggling around my eyes and down my arms. Suddenly, my body erupted into great pain. Alice appeared just as I saw a parasite crawl towards my heart. Alice was screaming, I was screaming, and Mr.Rumple was holding me like I was about to die. I couldn't breathe. The pain made me wish for the days while I was in The MEC. Every single tendon, muscle, and bone snapped, stretched, and broke. For a brief moment, my ribcage exploded and I could see my heart filled with millions of parasites. My ribcage fused back together and my entire body convulsed on the floor. Blood, snot, tears, and spittle formed a puddle around my body.

Mr.Rumple tried to catch Alice by her ears as my entire back bent into a 360-degree angle. My entire body twisted like a wet towel. Spots danced around my eyes. My body kept twisting to where it was barely recognizable. Bones were sticking out of my body like a voodoo doll. Alice bounced herself right onto my back as my body began to stretch itself back into its normal state. Sobbing, I hugged my body tightly. I was no longer Joannie, I was no longer Beauty. I was nothing more than the beast. A beast in love with the very man who was the biggest villain to walk the Earth. Everything went black as I felt weak. I collapsed on the floor shuddering as I closed my eyes.

I swirled alone in the darkness seeing and hearing nothing. I wanted to live with Mr.Rumple and feed off the bad people in the world. I had never wanted to live. Up to now, I didn't feel like I had much of a reason to live. When I had started this mission, I had hoped for death. Consuming Dilan, and having wild and amazing sex with Mr. Rumple would put me into an entirely different class.

When I woke up, the world had returned to the crap world it is today. The president was a rambling idiot making dementia-like decisions. People came back outside again, taking care of their lawns and themselves. It wasn't a perfect paradise. Gas prices skyrocketed, and people began to get angry. I tried to sit up but my head was killing me. I must have groaned loudly because Mr.Rumple came to the bedside.

"Welcome back. Are you ok?" He whispered as he stroked my cheek. "My head hurts and I feel like I am a little disjointed from my body," I whispered, my mouth was dry. Mr. Rumple brought me a glass of water and helped me sit up. My crystal arm was no longer crystallized. It looked like my normal arm but with thousands of scars on it. I looked in the mirror to see my black hair had several red streaks and had grown almost a foot. My eyes were not red crystals anymore. I looked almost normal again except for the scars.

"We did it! Let's go celebrate and go out to dinner." Mr. Rumple said with a boyish grin. I got dressed in my finest dress. We were walking hand in hand acting like a normal couple in love. Everything had resumed to the way it was before I took down The MECs. People were everywhere. Mr.Rumple and I sat down beside the lake that he had originally fallen in. When he fell into the polluted water, he had become Mr.Rumple. The polluted water danced and shimmered like a siren trying to lure in her prey. The moon was full and beautiful.

Mr. Rumple held me close as we whispered our plans on what we were going to do as we took over the world. Behind us, a twig snapped loudly. Whirling around, a woman stood there looking at us. She was dressed in a beautiful dark red dress, with a dark red lipstick match. She was holding a beautiful book that looked like the cover was bound with burnt flesh.

"Hello, Mr.Rumple and Beauty. It's been a while." The woman smiled. I wanted to ask her who she was, but she made my beauty pale in comparison to her. She walked up to us and offered us the book. With shaking hands, I took it and looked at the cover carefully. "Allisha, why are you here?" Mr. Rumple said with a death grip on my arm. My head snapped up. Allisha? As in Allisha McAdoo? I looked at the book cover again to see the title Beauty and Mr.Rumple.

"I am here simply because even though Dilan created you, I gave you your life. If I hadn't written about you, no one would have made a single deal with you. No one would have known who you are, or what you're capable of." When she walked, it was like she was floating just a little bit above the ground. "Now, Mr. Rumple gets the happy ending he always wanted is that right?" She asked. I still couldn't say anything at all. I was so captivated, that I couldn't breathe. "Yes, I want to make Beauty, my wife. We will only feed on the evil. I won't be a bother." Mr. Rumple said tightening his grip on my arm. "Tsk, tsk, tsk. Did you forget what your heart is now made of?" She laughed. There was something about her that could drive anyone crazy about her. "Your heart has the 13 souls of the evil." She said in a dangerously quiet voice. I noticed that on her right arm she had a strange marking up to her elbow. I turned to warn Mr. Rumple but it was too late. She grabbed him by his throat and said one word, "Omcanenorick" Mr. Rumple let out a scream as his entire body folded into a black pearl. The pearl Allisha put on her necklace and slipped it around her neck. The black pearl looked like an eye.

"Don't worry, Beauty, you will get him back when you can prove to me that you are a good person. You have devoured so much evil. If you want your love back, you will have to become a better person. This means you will blend in and be as human as you can. Only, then will I return Mr.Rumple to you." I was sobbing and suddenly I broke out of my trance. I took my fingernail and raked it across her neck as deep as I could go. She laughed, spit on her own finger, and wiped the wound shut. "You can't kill me. Better start trying to figure out how to be a better person. Because of all the power, you have consumed, eventually, your time will run out. You will go straight to hell that has been personally designed for you. I'll be around, writing and watching your every move." She slinked forward and kissed me on the mouth.

The kiss was sensual and almost made me forget that she had captured the love of my life. Damn Mr. Rumple for not taking care of her the last time. I leaned into the kiss feeling the black pearl touch my chest. When I opened my eyes, she was gone as well as Mr. Rumple.

So there you have it. That's my story. I am still trying to figure out how to ignore the fact that I want to eat people. I am trying to hide the fact that I am a monster and was enjoying being one. I am lonely and miss Mr.Rumple. I will find a way to break him free once more. He is my destiny. Whatever Allisha is doing to him, I will find a way to break him free. I will destroy her if it's the last thing I do. Game on. If I have to pretend to be human, I will also prepare for the war. I don't know what Allisha is, or why she is connected to Mr. Rumple the way she is, but mark my words, I will find out.

As she types my every thought I know she is smiling. This world is not strong enough for both of us to be in it. Another story for another day I suppose. This is far from over. I made myself a house that lies on the lake that first created that Mr. Rumple. Allisha now replaced my hatred and anger for Isaac.

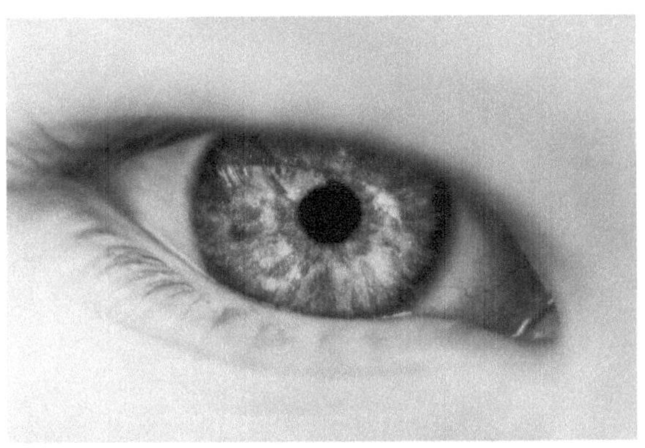

For right now............ The End..........

Authors Note

I really hope you enjoyed this story. I know it was a little farfetched and probably not edited right. Hopefully, you were able to see past that and enjoy it. :) Stay Tuned, more is to come, for Beauty and Mr. Rumple have more to come.